Sally Biddle appeared wearing a rose silk dress and a smug expression.

"Why, if it isn't Jane Peck! What a marvelous coincidence!" Sally trilled, her gold curls shining in the sun.

Jehu grinned at me, setting down the trunk he was carrying. "It'll be good to have an old friend out here, won't it, Jane?" I had never spoken to Jehu of Sally Biddle. In truth, I had hoped to forget her completely.

JENNIFER L. HOLM

BOSTON JANE
The Claim

📖 HARPERTROPHY®

An Imprint of HarperCollins*Publishers*

For my father, William Holm, M.D.,
and for my aunts, Elizabeth Holm and Louise Hunter.
Oysterman's kids, every one.

Harper Trophy® is a registered trademark of
HarperCollins Publishers Inc.

Boston Jane: The Claim
Copyright © 2004 by Jennifer L. Holm
For information address HarperCollins Children's Books,
a division of HarperCollins Publishers,
1350 Avenue of the Americas, New York, NY 10019.

Library of Congress Cataloging-in-Publication Data
Holm, Jennifer L.
   Boston Jane: the claim / Jennifer L. Holm.— 1st ed.
      p.   cm.
   Sequel to: Boston Jane : wilderness days.
   Summary: The arrival of her spiteful nemesis Sally Biddle from Philadelphia and the
return of her corrupt ex-fiance Richard Baldt spell trouble for seventeen-year-old Miss
Jane Peck, who has survived on her own in Shoalwater Bay, a community of white set-
tlers and Chinook Indians in 1850s Washington Territory.
   ISBN 0-06-029045-5 — ISBN 0-06-029046-3 (lib. bdg.)
   ISBN 0-06-440882-5 (pbk.)
   [1. Frontier and pioneer life—Washington (State)—Fiction. 2. Washington (State)—
History—To 1889—Fiction. 3. Orphans—Fiction. 4. Chinook Indians—Fiction. 5. Indians
of North America—Washington (State)—Fiction.] I. Title.
PZ7.H732226Br 2004   2003009556
[Fic]—dc21   CIP
                                                                         AC

❖
First Harper Trophy edition, 2005
Visit us on the World Wide Web!
www.harperchildrens.com

ACKNOWLEDGMENTS

As always, many thanks to all who have helped Jane Peck claim her place in the world.

For aiding me in my research, I would like to thank the usual suspects: Gary Johnson, Chairman of the Chinook Tribe; Bruce Weilepp of the Pacific County Historical Society; Joan Mann of the Ilwaco Heritage Museum; Paul and Ginny Merz; Elizabeth Holm, Matthew Holm, and my father, William Holm, M.D. And, of course, the wonderful Janet Frick.

A special thanks to my own sewing circle: Jill Applebaum, Shana Corey, Wendy Wilson, and Mercury Schroeppel.

I owe a great debt to Willard Espy, who so wonderfully chronicled his family's experiences on Shoalwater

Bay. And also to a girl after Jane's own heart, Louise Espy—a lady who went out to the wilderness and lived to tell about it.

Finally, a special thanks to the real Jehu Scudder for always making my coffee so perfectly.

In this privileged land, where we acknowledge

no distinctions but what are founded on character

and manners, she is a lady, who, to in-bred modesty

and refinement, adds a scrupulous attention

to the rights and feelings of others.

—THE YOUNG LADY'S FRIEND (1836),
By a Lady

or,

Old Ghosts

I was standing on a high bluff looking out at the vast shimmering sweep of blue-green water that was Shoalwater Bay.

Spring was in bloom, with drizzly rains and soft nights, and occasionally, a glorious day such as this one—when the sun broke out from behind the clouds and brushed the lush green wilderness with a golden tint. A sweet, salty wind swept over the waves, sending my thick, curly red hair flying in all directions. Gulls swooped and cried like nosy neighbors, diving low to the water. I should have been strolling through town, enjoying this rare and dazzling May day. Unfortunately, I was not feeling very well.

As a matter of fact, I was puking.

I had thought she was a ghost, perched behind Jehu

in the back of a rowboat heading toward shore. I *wished* she were a ghost.

I retched again, but there was nothing left in my stomach.

Sally Biddle. With her wealthy family and faultless manners, she had been the belle of Philadelphia society when I lived there. But beneath her blond ringlets and fashionable gowns, she was a perfect monster, one whose chief amusement was tormenting other girls. Or at least one girl. Me. She had contrived to make my childhood a misery. And whenever I had earned small victories, Sally had always made me pay for them tenfold.

Trust me, you would puke, too.

Sally was one of the reasons I had been so eager to leave Philadelphia to put an entire continent between us. And now, here she was. What possible reason could my childhood tormentor have for following me to the farthest reaches of the Washington Territory? It made no sense. Had she traveled all this way just to torture me?

But there was no denying it. She was real. No ghost would wear such an elegant dress with a matching cape and smart bonnet. Why, Sally looked as if she were on her way to tea, and not arriving from a sea voyage of several months. She looked perfect, as usual, not at all like the sad sack I had been upon my arrival more than a year earlier.

When Jehu's rowboat had hit the sandy beach, the sick feeling in the pit of my stomach exploded, and a single thought thrummed in my head:

Sally Biddle is here!

Sally had stood up and held out a hand to Jehu, and the sight of that gloved hand resting on Jehu's strong arm as he helped her to shore had shaken me like nothing else could. I had done the only thing a lady could do in such a situation. I had picked up my skirts and run all the way up here to the high bluff to be sick in private.

Now, with each breath of crisp air, I felt my stomach settle and a measure of calm return to me. I was on *my claim*, I told myself over and over, like a litany. Behind me was the beginning of the beautiful new home my sweet Jehu was building me. Nothing bad could happen to me here.

Something in the distance caught my eye. A blond-haired figure was slowly strolling through the woods, pausing here and there. At first glance I feared Sally Biddle had followed me, but then I saw that it was clearly a man, and not a lady.

"Boston Jane!" a voice cried from the other direction.

I turned to see little Sootie and her cousin Katy barreling toward me, dolls in tow. When I looked back to where the figure had been, he was gone, vanished into the thick dark woods.

"We've been looking everywhere for you!" Sootie exclaimed in a rush.

Sootie was a whirligig of energy. With her thick black hair, copper skin, and bright, excited eyes, the daughter of Chief Toke of the Chinook tribe took after her mother, my friend Suis, who had died in the smallpox epidemic the previous year.

"Star's has new fabric! It just arrived on the schooner!" she exclaimed in a rush, waving her rag doll at me.

Sootie, like her mother before her, was a skilled trader, and she had amassed a small collection of dolls from other children of the settlement through her skillful dealings. I had promised her that I would make a dress for this latest doll.

"Why are you all the way out here?" Katy asked curiously.

Katy, the eleven-year-old daughter of a local pioneer and his Chinook wife, had inherited the fair skin of her father and the brown eyes and lustrous black hair of her mother. She was an uncommonly beautiful little girl with a gentle disposition that I found charming.

"I'm hiding from a *memelose*," I said lightly.

"A *memelose*?" Katy asked in hushed tones, looking around nervously. "Really?"

Memelose was the Chinook word for spirit.

"You should change your name, Boston Jane," Sootie said, all seriousness. "Then the *memelose* won't be able to find you."

The Chinook believed that if you changed your

name, you could outwit a *memelose* who wanted to lure you to the other side. And in a manner of speaking, I had done just that. I was now known to many here on the bay as Boston Jane, a name bestowed upon me by my Chinook friends and dear to me for what it implied. Boston Jane was a woman of courage. She had survived and endured in the wilderness, carving a place for herself in this fragile settlement at the edge of the frontier. But I knew that I could change my name a thousand times and it would not alter the fact that Sally Biddle was here on Shoalwater Bay.

"The *memelose* has already found me," I said.

Sootie considered this for a moment, then declared bravely, "I'm not afraid of *memeloses*!"

I wanted to tell her that Sally Biddle was one *memelose* she should fear.

"Don't worry, Boston Jane," Katy said. "We'll protect you!"

"She's not really a *memelose*," I admitted. "She's just a girl." A rather disagreeable girl, I wanted to add.

"You can tell us the truth, Boston Jane. We're not afraid," Katy said.

"I wish she weren't real," I murmured.

They nodded.

"Now come to town," Sootie said, tugging at my arm. "Before all the fabric is gone!"

I looked out at the sparkling bay and sighed. I couldn't very well hide forever, could I? I brushed off my hands on my skirt, tugged my bonnet over my wild red curls, and stood up.

"Very well," I agreed, and then gave them a small wink. "But if Sally Biddle comes to haunt me, I'm sending her after you!"

Mr. Russell's raggedy little cabin marked the far edge of our burgeoning settlement.

Pioneers came to Shoalwater Bay lured by stories of oyster farming, and land for homesteading. Our town was growing right along the shore, making it most convenient for the hardworking oystermen who toiled on the bay. Many of the homes were built on pilings and floats to survive the sometimes perilously high tides. In some places the cabins were scarcely more than shacks, and tents were visible as well. While there were several families in residence now, most of our inhabitants were unmarried men, which was why, I supposed, we had three taverns and a coffin shop but no schools.

Mr. Russell's cabin, though, was sensibly placed far above the high-water mark, in a clearing in the woods. When I'd first arrived, this ramshackle cabin was the only true house the settlement had to offer. It was my first home here. Unfortunately, it had also been home to every filthy, flea-bitten prospecting man who happened to be passing through. Mr. Russell was not generally given to cleanliness, and his cabin usually reflected this personal trait. At the moment, the bewhiskered, buckskin-clad mountain man was sitting on the porch.

"Hello, Mr. Russell," I called, and waved.

He spit a wad of tobacco in my general direction and waved back to us.

Mr. Russell and I had been through a lot together, and I felt a tremendous fondness for the man. I'll admit I even felt a bit homesick for that wretched dirt-floor shack of his.

The girls and I passed the cabin and set off along the main road that led down to the center of town. I was immediately barraged by the familiar scents and sounds that characterized Front Street—raucous shouts emanating from one of the taverns, the tangy smell of manure mixed with mud, the sharp salty breeze off the bay, oystermen dickering over prices, the murmurs of men discussing whether or not it would rain.

Front Street, which ran parallel to shore, was a rather grand title for a path that was usually little more than a swath of thick, boot-sticking mud. A ramshackle, narrow walkway, constructed of spare planks salvaged from shipwrecks and packing crates, ran alongside this muddy route. My young companions ran nimbly along the walkway, dancing ahead of me.

"Hurry, Boston Jane," Sootie shouted over her shoulder. "All the fabric will be gone!"

Front Street was crowded with all manner of men.

There were Indians from local tribes, pioneers from back east, miners who had not struck gold in California and wanted to try their chances on oysters, and men who were fleeing the law. In short, our citizens consisted mainly of rough-and-tumble men who could not be bothered to build proper houses or bathe but happily drank their earnings. It was altogether a wild community, especially after dark.

Wagons full of freshly harvested oysters hauled their cargo up and down the muddy thoroughfare. Here and there, men were holding friendly wagers by tossing gold coins in the sand. Oysters were making men rich. The native bivalves were in such demand in San Francisco that men thought nothing of paying a silver dollar for a fresh-shucked oyster.

Even I was part of the oyster rush. I owned a canoe and oyster beds with my friend Mr. Swan, although our business had not been too successful of late. My partner had gambled away the profits from the last harvest. As I was increasingly busy with my duties at the hotel where I worked, I was considering renting out the beds to another oysterman for a share of the profits.

Ahead of me a man stood lounging on the narrow walkway, making it impossible for me to pass.

"Excuse me," I said.

But the man, who had clearly been spending his oyster money on whiskey, simply leered at me.

I was forced to step onto the road, where I soon

found myself ankle-deep in mud. After several boot-clogging steps, I passed the man and climbed back onto the walkway.

Farther down the muddy thoroughfare, I spied the gay bunting of Star's Dry Goods, and beyond that the outline of the Frink Hotel.

Sootie bounded up the steps of Star's in front of me, while Katy hovered behind.

"Boston Jane, what if the *memelose* girl is here?" Katy asked in a whisper. "*Memeloses* are very dangerous! They can hurt you because no one can see them."

"We'll be fine," I assured her with more courage than I felt.

She eyed me warily.

A small brass bell attached to the door rang as we entered.

Star's Dry Goods was a jumble of goods stacked floor to ceiling. There were harness fittings, bird seed, molasses, nails, flour, tea, coffee, and even umbrellas—the most practical item in the store considering the amount of rain Shoalwater Bay received. The huge barrel of molasses sat alongside a barrel of hard cider and one of vinegar. Glass jars filled with candy waited hopefully for small children to sample their wares. In addition to the standard store items, Mr. Staroselsky's wife ordered goods that were appreciated by the ladies. There was a very nice assortment of fabrics, as well as sewing needles, ribbon, buttons, hosiery, cotton yarns, and combs. It was all arranged in a haphazard fashion that only Mr. Staroselsky seemed to know how to navigate.

In the back of the room, several men sat in captain's chairs around the small potbellied stove. It was a favorite place to exchange gossip.

"Hello, Jane," Mrs. Staroselsky called from behind the counter.

Mrs. Staroselsky, a vibrant young woman with a tumble of thick, black curly hair, could often be seen making deliveries around town for her husband. She had a brand-new baby named Rose, who was presently in her arms and making quite a fuss.

Sootie pushed in front of me to the counter. "Boston Jane is going to buy us some of the new fabric for our dolls!"

"For new dresses!" Katy added.

"Well, aren't you girls lucky," Mrs. Staroselsky said, smiling at me over Sootie's head. "I saw Jehu with an enormous wagon of luggage. New arrivals?"

Jehu acted as the pilot for the bay, guiding ships in through the shoals and helping them unload their goods.

"Yes," I said. "From Philadelphia."

"How wonderful for you to have folks here from back home," Mrs. Staroselsky said.

I bit my lip.

"Can I hold the baby?" Sootie asked, scrambling up

to peer at the whimpering baby in Mrs. Staroselsky's arms.

"You may," Mrs. Staroselsky said, passing her the restless bundle. "Perhaps you can calm her down. She's been crying for days."

I nodded sympathetically.

"Look, she's not crying anymore!" Sootie said in a hushed voice as she carefully rocked the baby. "She likes me!"

And indeed, Rose was staring up at Sootie's face with something approaching wonder.

Mrs. Staroselsky and I smiled over the girls' heads.

"Maybe you should keep Rose for a while, Sootie," Mrs. Staroselsky said with a wink.

I left Sootie and Katy at Star's, minding the baby, and continued down Front Street toward the Frink Hotel, passing one of the local taverns, which doubled as a bowling alley.

The tavern was situated inside an abandoned Chinook lodge, and shouting and revelry could be heard there until all hours of the night. Men seemed to lose all good sense when whiskey was involved, and there was a great deal of whiskey available on Shoalwater Bay, thanks to Red Charley. Red Charley had grown rich in his whiskey dealings and liked to go about town with a woolen sock full of gold coins tied to his belt. The whiskey-dealing devil himself was lolling outside the bowling alley on an empty barrel as I walked by.

"Lookee there," Red Charley chortled. "It's Jane Peck! When're you gonna get rid of that sailor fella, huh?"

Red Charley was referring to Jehu, who was a seasoned sailor and captain. He had been first mate on the *Lady Luck*, the ship that had brought me to Shoalwater Bay.

Red Charley turned to the filthy prospecting fellow lazing next to him and said, "I keep telling her I'll marry her! What does Jehu got that I don't?" He followed his question with a belch. "I sure am a lot more handsome."

I raised an eyebrow at this. With his huge belly, red cheeks, and terrible disposition, Red Charley was hardly a young lady's dream.

"How's he going to support you puttering around in that wee boat?" another man shouted.

"How do ya know he hasn't got a wife in some other port? Now an oysterman like me'll stay put," a man with a missing tooth assured me with a lopsided smile.

"He ain't worth love," Red Charley cackled. "The only thing worth that kind of hankering is Old Rye!"

"Good day," I said firmly, and continued on, dragging my now muddy skirts behind me.

Farther down the street I arrived at the Frink Hotel. Outside it stood a horse-drawn wagon piled high with trunks, and helping to unload the wagon was the dark-haired sailor Red Charley had been talking about.

"Jehu!" I called happily.

He turned to me, his eyes lighting up, his smile tugging at my heart. He was so handsome with his shock of curly black hair, his blue eyes, the scar that ran jaggedly along his cheek.

"Jane," he said.

At that moment the door to the hotel opened and Sally Biddle appeared, wearing a rose silk dress and a smug expression.

"Why, if it isn't Jane Peck! What a marvelous coincidence!" Sally trilled, her gold curls shining in the sun.

Jehu grinned at me, setting down the trunk he was carrying. "It'll be good to have an old friend out here, won't it, Jane?"

I had never spoken to Jehu of Sally Biddle. In truth, I had hoped to forget her completely.

"Yes, Jane. I was just telling Mr. Scudder what *great* friends we were in Philadelphia," Sally said sweetly, the very model of a kind girlfriend, her gaze lingering just a moment too long on Jehu's handsome features. "We had such wonderful times together, didn't we?"

I saw the look in Sally's eyes daring me to contradict her, and my stomach roiled. Katy was right to have warned me. Sally Biddle was just as dangerous as any *memelose*—and no one but me could see her true self. I felt my face go cold, my skin prickle with sweat.

"Jane," Sally said, her eyes mock-solicitous. "Are you

feeling well? You look rather . . . *drawn*."

"Jane?" Jehu asked, concern in his voice.

But I couldn't answer. I turned and fled up the stairs of the hotel to my room.

or,

The Most Important Lesson

As I stared at my pale face in the mirror, the past came rushing back.

At twelve I had worked hard to be accepted into Miss Hepplewhite's Young Ladies Academy, one of the best finishing schools in all of Philadelphia. Miss Hepplewhite taught her students the finer points of being a proper young lady. Her lessons ranged from such social niceties as Pouring Tea and Coffee, and Deportment at the Dinner Table, to Receiving and Returning Calls, and Being a Good Guest. But by far the most important lesson I had learned was Never Underestimate Sally Biddle.

From the day I entered Miss Hepplewhite's, Sally did her best to isolate me from the other girls, and she generally succeeded. Nevertheless, at the age of fifteen,

I received, after years of hoping, a coveted invitation to Cora Fletcher's exclusive Midsummer Gala. An invitation to the annual Fletcher ball was an open door to acceptance in society. It was proof that, despite Sally Biddle's efforts to the contrary, I could finally *belong*.

Mary, my maid, and Mrs. Parker, the housekeeper who had filled in all my life for the mother I lost the day I was born, spent two weeks helping me prepare what I would wear to the ball. On the eve of the big event, I arrived at the Fletchers' house in my new gown.

The drawing room was full of young ladies and gentlemen dressed in their best, and I felt beautiful in my pale green satin dress with its demure bows ringing the hem, and one at each shoulder.

Sally appeared at my side, offering me a cup of punch. I was pleased, thinking that she wanted to make peace with me.

I was most mistaken.

For I had no sooner taken the cup than Sally brushed past me to speak to another guest and shoved me hard with her elbow. The glass tipped, and punch soaked the bosom of my dress and dripped down my skirts, and that was the end of my gala evening.

But now as I gazed into the mirror in my room at the hotel, I knew I wasn't looking at the same girl Sally had known in Philadelphia. The girl who had arrived on the *Lady Luck* hadn't known how to bake a pie, let alone survive in the wilderness. I had grown and changed and was no longer the kind of person to give up without a fight. I was no longer a child. I was seventeen years old and had in the past few months both survived a bear attack and outwitted a ruthless murderer. Truly, what was Sally Biddle compared to all that? I thought with a rush of confidence.

I turned away from the mirror, resolved not to be afraid of this old *memelose*, and headed down the hall— only to catch sight of Sally Biddle disappearing around a corner. I wondered for a moment if I would have preferred a grizzly bear after all.

Grizzly bears at least had the decency to put you out of your misery.

I passed Mr. Frink on the back stairs, hauling a huge trunk. His forehead was drenched with sweat as he struggled with his heavy burden.

"Is that the last one?" I asked.

"Six more to go," he said with a groan.

A pretty young woman with rosy cheeks and laughing eyes met me as I stepped into the parlor. Mrs. Frink was the proprietress of the Frink Hotel and my dear friend. I credited the swift construction of the hotel to her. She had a singular talent for charming people into doing any manner of things. Matilda was easily the most competent lady I had ever made acquaintance with in my entire life. I adored her in spite of it.

"Oh Jane, I do hope my Mr. Frink doesn't hurt

his back carrying up all those trunks," Mrs. Frink exclaimed. Her voice lowered to a confiding whisper. "The young lady of the family had ten trunks alone. I daresay Miss Biddle bought out all of Philadelphia before coming here!"

I wasn't the least bit surprised that Sally had brought so many clothes. Fine clothes were a necessity for a wealthy young woman hoping to make a good match. Not that anyone had ever doubted for a moment Sally's ability to make a good match.

Mr. Frink came trudging down the stairs, looking weary.

He was a mild-mannered man who rarely had a word to say. But he looked up the stairs and whispered, "You reckon they packed a cookstove in one of those trunks?"

"They seem very nice people," Mrs. Frink said.

Mr. Frink was scratching his head. "Do you know they brought silver for twenty? Twenty! Now who do you reckon they're gonna serve dinner to with that?"

"Jane, Miss Biddle was just telling me what great friends you were in Philadelphia," Mrs. Frink said, a trace of curiosity in her voice.

"We weren't exactly friends," I hedged. "More like acquaintances. We attended the same school. Did she happen to mention what brought them to Shoalwater Bay?"

"Not a word, my dear. But it must be a comfort to

you to see a familiar face. Sometimes when I think of all the friends I left in Ohio . . ." Mrs. Frink's expression grew wistful, then changed again as if she'd had a flash of inspiration. "Why don't you make one of your famous pies this evening? You know, as a special touch to welcome them to the hotel?"

"Of course," I said.

"That would be lovely!" Mrs. Frink clapped her hands. "Now, Jane, if you would be so kind as to look in on supper, I shall make sure our new guests are settled!" She bustled off.

The Frink Hotel was one of the establishments that had opened this spring to the delight of residents and arriving settlers. It was by far the grandest building in Shoalwater Bay. Which is to say it was the only structure that was more than one story.

Guests of the Frink Hotel were generally not as refined as the Biddles. While we had the occasional family who boarded with us while their own cabin was being built, the hotel catered mostly to oystermen. In fact, so many of our guests were oystermen that we accepted oysters in lieu of payment. A dry place to sleep was now in such demand that rooms originally meant for one man had been reconfigured with sleeping bunks so that up to four men shared a single room. Oystermen who could not obtain a bed at the Frink Hotel had been known to sleep in all manner of places: hollowed-out trees, empty barrels, and even—as Mr.

Frink discovered one morning—the privy!

The hotel was a great success, and its mere existence lent prestige to our young community. The Frinks' generosity was legendary. If a man was down on his luck and unable to pay his bill, he would not be ushered out of the hotel at gunpoint, as was the case in many establishments. Rather, he would find a small bag of coins under his pillow in the morning. If a man became ill, he was not turned out onto the street, but was allowed to remain at the hotel, and was often nursed by Mrs. Frink herself. Because of this, Mrs. Frink and her husband were much admired by all the residents of Shoalwater Bay, and never was an unkind word uttered about either of them.

As concierge it was my responsibility to order supplies and organize the daily menus, as well as manage the day-to-day business of the hotel. In addition to offering accommodations, the hotel served breakfast and supper. The men, most of them bachelors, were more than happy to have a cooked meal, and so the hotel also was a very popular—in fact, the *only*—establishment for supper. Due to this great demand, I would also lend a hand in the kitchen on occasion.

We employed several people to help run the hotel. There was my friend Spaark, who worked in the kitchen; a woman named Millie, who cleaned the rooms and cooked; and a boy named Willard Woodley, who was supposed to help in the kitchen but who more often than not was missing. Mr. Frink was responsible for repairs, and Jehu helped with the luggage and anything else requiring heavy lifting. Mrs. Dodd, a local pioneer woman, took in the laundry. And there was also Brandywine, a dog, whose chief contribution was eating scraps of food dropped on the kitchen floor.

When I went in to see about the pie, the kitchen was a hot, steamy hive of activity. Spaark and Millie were already hard at work.

"It looks as if we shall have a full room for supper," I said. "As usual."

"Pretty dress, Boston Jane," Keer-ukso, one of my Chinook friends, said flirtatiously. He was lounging in a corner of the kitchen. "Maybe I marry you if you wear that dress!"

Keer-ukso was incredibly handsome, with thick black hair and a finely muscled body. His old name, before he changed it to Keer-ukso, had suited him perfectly: Handsome Jim. Young women had a tendency to trail after him, although he paid them little attention, for the only young lady who mattered to him these days was the one across the kitchen stirring a kettle of oyster stew: Spaark.

"Boston Jane is too smart to marry you," Spaark said, rolling her eyes at me.

She was a young lady from the neighboring Chehalis tribe, and we had grown to be close friends in the past months as we worked together at the hotel. I had met her at a meeting of the local tribes the previous winter, and she and Keer-ukso had taken a liking to each other. The two of them were now courting, and she lived at Chief Toke's lodge. She had a marvelous sense of humor and kept Keer-ukso on his toes.

"Boston Jane, you not marry me?" Keer-ukso gave a mock-wounded look, but I saw the sparkle in his eyes.

"Shouldn't you be off helping Jehu instead of getting in the way?" I said, batting him toward the door.

"Jehu is fine by himself," Keer-ukso said.

"Well, then you can stay and help with supper," I suggested. "I see that Willard is missing as usual, and I'm sure that Spaark and Millie would welcome the help, wouldn't you, ladies?"

Keer-ukso didn't look the least bit affronted. "I am better cook than Spaark or you!" Among the Chinook, it was quite common for the men to cook as well as the women.

"Wonderful!" I said, pointing to a bucket. "The oysters need to be shucked."

Millie grinned and held up an enormous sack of potatoes. "And the potatoes peeled."

Spaark followed suit. "And the dishes washed!"

Keer-ukso looked aghast, waving his hands in front of him defensively. He beat a hasty retreat out the back door.

Spaark shook her head at him affectionately, and we all laughed.

"Splendid. Now if I can only find Willard," I said, casting a glance out the back door of the kitchen, "I can set him to work peeling potatoes."

Ten-year-old Willard Woodley was the only son of a recently arrived family, and he was a true rascal. His mother had asked me if I would hire him, as he had rather abruptly quit his job assisting the laundress, Mrs. Dodd. There was always a surfeit of work around the hotel, so I was happy to oblige her. Unfortunately, Willard had the uncanny ability to disappear when there was any real work to be done.

I poked my head out the kitchen door. "Willard?"

Silence was my answer.

"Willard," I called. "I just finished baking a pie and thought you might enjoy a slice."

Spaark grinned mischievously at me.

"It's still warm from the oven," I continued in a loud voice. "And it looks just delicious, doesn't it, Spaark?"

"Oh yes," Spaark said, playing along with my little game. "I will have pie, too."

Just then, a pair of eyes topped off by a mop of blond hair peered in the doorway.

"Willard, how lovely to see you!" I exclaimed in delight.

Willard came creeping into the kitchen, eyes scanning the worktables for pie. Hot on the boy's heels was a black, potbellied dog. It was Brandywine, longtime resident of Shoalwater Bay. Brandywine and Willard were inseparable nowadays, probably because they could always count on each other to find something tasty.

"Where's the pie?" Willard asked suspiciously.

I crossed my arms in front of me. "Actually, Willard, I am just about to make the pie, but I promise to put aside a nice slice for you."

The boy's face fell.

"In the meantime, I would very much appreciate it if you'd take this bowl of potatoes and peel them out back," I said firmly.

"I s'pose so," he said reluctantly, shoulders slumped. He took the bowl and slunk from the kitchen, Brandywine trailing behind him, equally disappointed.

"That's the last time that little trick works," I murmured, tying on an apron.

Across the room Millie was stacking dishes, counting them out carefully. Like me, she lived at the hotel. Originally from New Hampshire, she and her husband had traveled to Oregon, intending to homestead some land. They had no sooner arrived when her husband got it into his head that he wanted to try his hand at the gold mines in California. By all accounts he left her with little more than a tent to protect her from the elements, promising to return a rich man. That was nearly three years ago.

Mr. Russell had met her when he was on a buying trip in Astoria, across the Columbia River in Oregon, and told her that Mrs. Frink was looking for help. A week later Millie had appeared at the front door of the hotel—a thin woman with sad eyes.

"I'm a good worker," she had said simply.

She never spoke of her husband. I knew all too well what she had suffered, for I had experienced something like it myself. I had traveled from Philadelphia to Shoalwater Bay to marry Dr. William Baldt, a former apprentice of my father's. When I had arrived after a sea journey of several months, he was not to be found in the territory and had left no word for me. I had been forced to make my way on my wits, without a man to support or help me.

Millie seemed to think her husband would one day return. I could see it in her eyes, the way she looked up when a door opened, how she scanned the faces of the men who filed in for supper. She was endlessly kind to the rough-and-tumble men, even mending their filthy socks. It was clear that she missed having a man of her own to look after, and I'll confess to a little matchmaking.

"Millie," I said. "Have you met the gentleman who arrived yesterday? The one staying in the back room upstairs?"

A jovial-looking oysterman had taken a room in the hotel, and something about the kindness in his eyes made me think he might be good for Millie. "He seems very agreeable," I continued.

Millie shook her head, which was what she always did when confronted with these attempts on my part. Spaark met my eyes and gave a slight shrug.

"I'm a married woman," Millie said.

"What if he never comes back?" I asked softly.

Millie stared down at her plates, and when she glanced back up, there was a hollow look in her eyes.

"Then I'm still a married woman," she whispered.

Hotel guests were called to meals by a bell. A hearty breakfast was served promptly at seven, and supper at six. There was always hot coffee available for a weary man who had come in from his oyster beds, and Millie was occasionally known to set out a late-night snack for hungry men. Mealtime was a boisterous affair, and the men ate whatever was put in front of them with incredible speed. A meal that took Spaark, Millie, and me the better part of the day to prepare was often dispatched within less than fifteen minutes! Still, we had learned to take this as a compliment.

The dining room was arranged with the largest table at one end, and the other, smaller tables positioned around the room. The largest table was known as the head table, and this was where the Frinks took their supper, as did I. Mrs. Frink was a marvelous conversationalist, and dining at the head table was considered a treat. It was also, unfortunately, where I found myself seated that evening along with Sally and her parents, and another couple, the Hosmers.

"So, Mr. Biddle," Mrs. Frink said, and then asked the very question I was wondering myself. "What brings you to our fair Shoalwater Bay?"

Mr. Biddle was plump and short, and the suit he wore strained at the seams. Clearly the sea voyage had not disagreed with him. If anything, he looked heavier than I recalled. His face had a rather squashed appearance, and his eyes seemed fixed in a perpetual look of dismay, or was it a frown? It was hard to say exactly, but altogether he resembled a small, irritable dog with a tuft of hair poking out of the top of his head.

"I understand there are a number of investment opportunities in this part of the frontier," Mr. Biddle said.

"Are you interested in getting into oysters?" I asked, my curiosity near to bursting.

"Actually," he said, "my interests lie more in land speculation."

"How fascinating," Mrs. Frink said. "You must speak with our Jane. She has been here longer than any of us and knows the bay the best!"

Mrs. Hosmer turned to Sally and said, her admiration plain, "That's a very fetching dress, Miss Biddle."

Mrs. Hosmer, who was just a few years my senior, had arrived with her equally youthful husband from New York after the new year. Even though they lived in a cabin down the muddy road, they took all their meals at the hotel. Apparently Mrs. Hosmer didn't know how to cook. How they had survived the wagon-train journey was anyone's guess, but her new husband seemed quite infatuated with his beautiful young wife.

"Why, thank you. I just had it copied from *Godey's Lady's Book*," Sally said with a modest smile. With a daring neckline that left her slim shoulders bare, I had no doubt that the dress Sally was wearing had been a highlight of the premier fashion magazine for ladies. More than one filthy oysterman had ceased shoveling food into his mouth and stared at her when she entered the dining room.

"How I miss *Godey's*!" Mrs. Hosmer said with a trace of longing in her voice.

"But you must borrow my copies then," Sally said. "And please call me Sally."

I watched this byplay with a trace of irritation. Sally clearly had not left her social skills behind in Philadelphia!

A burly, filthy man at a table directly behind Mrs. Biddle turned around and tapped her on the shoulder.

"Pardon me, ma'am," he rasped. "But would you kindly pass me the salt."

She stared at him for a long moment and then turned her back, ignoring his request.

"Well, I ain't never," he said.

Millie whisked the salt off the head table and deposited it in front of the man.

Mr. Biddle cleared his throat elaborately, as if preparing to launch into an oration. "Miss Peck. We were very sorry to learn of your father's death," he said, and I started.

My father had been a surgeon in Philadelphia, and he had been much admired by all of society. He had belonged to the same club as Mr. Biddle. No doubt Mr. Biddle had seen Papa before his death, long after I had left Philadelphia. I felt tears prick behind my eyes.

"Did Papa"—I hesitated—"did he say anything? I mean—"

"Actually," Mr. Biddle replied, "your father and I discussed my intention to come out here at some length. Before he died, James asked me to look in on you, and see how you and William were faring out here." Mr. Biddle paused. "So, how are you faring?"

I looked around the table at the expectant faces. Sally's gaze was focused on my finger—where no wedding ring rested.

"I am doing quite well, actually," I said.

Mrs. Biddle, who was seated on my right, turned to me and said in a critical tone, "The food certainly seems to agree with you."

I knew very well what Mrs. Biddle meant by this. Being slender and pale was all the rage back east, but I no longer subscribed to such fashion. As for Mrs. Biddle, she was the very image of the ideal Philadelphia lady, with her thin waist and ashen complexion. I rather wondered if the pained look on her face was from the tightness of her corset or from finding herself at the edge of the frontier, far from Philadelphia society.

Mrs. Biddle lowered her voice to a loud whisper. "Are you not wearing a corset?"

"No," I whispered back. I had disposed of the confining garment some time ago.

She shook her head in dismay.

"Where do you live, Jane?" Sally asked.

Jehu was building my house with the help of Keer-ukso. The three of us had designed it together over the spring, and I could hardly wait until it was finished. Finally I would have a home again, a place to call my very own. It had been rather slow going, as there wasn't a proper sawmill on the bay, although Jehu and Keer-ukso hoped to remedy that soon by opening one of their own. My two dearest friends here had become fast friends themselves and would soon be business partners as well.

"I'm living here while my house is being built," I said.

"I see. And where is your handsome husband?" Sally asked.

Mrs. Hosmer looked at me with a confused expression. "You're married?"

"Actually," I said, "I didn't marry William."

Sally looked as if she were going to burst into laughter. I had expected just such a reaction from her.

Mr. Biddle seemed perplexed. "Didn't marry him? That's the first I've heard of this."

"Papa," Sally said, her voice tinged with amusement. "A lady has a right to change her mind."

Change my mind? I hadn't changed my mind. When he finally appeared in the area many weeks after my arrival, William had already been married to another woman. So while I had technically broken off the engagement, it wasn't for some flight of fancy.

Sally turned to me, her eyes alight with mischief. She was clearly enjoying my revelation. "No doubt there are lots of eligible bachelors out here, Jane."

Before I could answer, Mrs. Biddle said in a horrified voice, "Do you mean that you have been living here, in the wilderness, *unescorted*, all this time?"

In good society it was considered the height of impropriety for an unmarried young lady to live unescorted. Unfortunately, I hadn't had much choice in the matter. My dear friend and companion, Mary, had died on the voyage here.

"There are quite a number of ladies here now," I said.

"Well," Mrs. Biddle sniffed. "It sounds most irregular."

"Were you and Sally friends back in Philadelphia?" Mrs. Hosmer asked.

"Why, yes!" Sally said in a gay voice. "The very best of friends, weren't we, Jane?"

"How nice for you, Jane," Mrs. Hosmer said, sounding a bit envious. "To have a dear friend here on the frontier."

"Oh, but I should very much like to be your friend, Mrs. Hosmer," Sally said.

Mrs. Hosmer looked delighted. "You are terribly kind, Miss Biddle."

I almost groaned.

"By the way, Jane," Sally said, "Cora Fletcher asked me to send you her regards. Her Midsummer Gala was quite a success this year."

"Really," I said in a flat voice.

Her eyes fairly sparkled as she murmured, "The punch was just delicious!"

or,

The Sewing Circle

After supper that evening Mr. Hosmer quietly took me aside in the hallway and asked me if I wouldn't mind giving his new wife lessons in cookery.

"Your pies sure are good, Miss Peck. And my wife, bless her heart, well, she just doesn't have the knack. Way I figure, if you maybe taught her how to cook, we could eat meals in our own cabin once in a while," he finished with a sheepish grin.

"I'd be happy to," I said, smiling.

Judging by her faultless manners, Mrs. Hosmer had no doubt received an education similar to mine, and my schooling had proved impractical in most respects. It was all very well to know the difference between a salad fork and a fish fork, but what did it matter when the preferred method was using one's fingers, as was the Chinook custom?

The next morning I made good on my promise. I pulled on my bonnet and headed over to the Hosmers' cabin, carrying a basket that contained a jar of preserved cherries. Mrs. Parker's receipt for cherry pie was quite simple. The secret ingredient was a pinch of cinnamon.

The Hosmers lived at the far end of Front Street, next to Mrs. Dodd, the laundress. The harsh smell of lye rising from great cauldrons of boiling water filled the air as I passed the Dodds' yard.

"Miss Peck, how kind of you to pay me a call!" Mrs. Hosmer exclaimed when she opened her door. "Do come in."

She ushered me in and bade me take a seat, but I wasn't sure where. Every surface was cluttered with all manner of garbage.

In addition to not knowing how to cook, Mrs. Hosmer apparently didn't know how to keep house either, for the cabin was a disaster. Laundry was piled high everywhere, and clumps of mud crisscrossed the floor. The bed hadn't been made, and the fire was cold. Dirty dishes were stacked precariously in a bucket, and there was a strange smell emanating from under a pile of rags in the corner.

"Please excuse the mess," Mrs. Hosmer began. "Mr. Hosmer has promised to find me a maid, but apparently good help is rather scarce on the bay."

"Mrs. Hosmer," I said, placing my basket on the table and pulling out the jar of preserved cherries. "I thought we might bake a pie together."

"A pie?" Mrs. Hosmer said, sounding dumbfounded.

"Yes," I said. "A cherry pie."

She looked at me as if she thought I'd quite lost my mind. "Miss Peck, why would I want to do that?"

She reminded me so much of myself when I'd first arrived on the bay. Like her, I had been a proper young lady who knew how to embroider and pour tea and dance perfectly, but I hadn't known the first thing about cooking or building a fire or anything that involved real work. And at the time I had seen no reason to learn.

I tried a different tack. "It's just that all the ladies on the bay know how to bake, and sometimes we exchange receipts."

"Oh, I see. This is considered social here, to bake?" she asked.

"Precisely," I said. "I suspect your husband would love to come home to a pie. It is a very romantic gesture."

"He *does* like cherry pie," she mused. "But it would be ever so much easier if there were a baker nearby."

"Wonderful," I said. "Let's get started."

I dug around and finally found a half-clean bowl and wooden spoon.

"We'll make the crust first. I'll need some flour.

Where do you keep it?" I asked.

Mrs. Hosmer looked about the cabin. "I don't recall seeing any lately. My husband usually takes care of those sorts of things."

"I suppose I could run back to the hotel and fetch some. But we'll need lard as well."

"Lard?" Mrs. Hosmer sounded puzzled by the request.

"What about pie tins?" I asked.

She gave a bewildered shrug.

In the end, Mrs. Hosmer watched. She watched as I ran over to Star's to buy flour and lard. She watched as I ran back to the hotel to borrow pie tins and cinnamon. She watched as I fetched wood and built a fire. And she watched as I sorted her laundry, and washed all her dishes, and swept the cabin, and put fresh sheets on the bed.

By the time I finished, the scent of baking pie filled the air, the cabin was neat as a pin, and I was ready to drop.

"I'm so exhausted, Miss Peck, after all this work," Mrs. Hosmer said dramatically. "But this was very enjoyable."

Just then Mr. Hosmer stepped into the cabin, his eyes widening in delight. "Something sure smells good."

Mrs. Hosmer beamed at her husband. "I've been hard at work all morning, darling!"

"You've done a great job, sweetheart," he said,

placing a gentle kiss on her forehead. "Hasn't she, Miss Peck?"

"She sure has," I said weakly.

After wasting the better part of my morning trying to teach Mrs. Hosmer, I returned to the hotel to change into a fresh dress, then set about organizing things for the sewing circle that afternoon. It was my turn to act as hostess, and I planned to serve tea and jam tarts.

Even though it was called the sewing circle, we didn't actually seem to get any sewing done, preferring to gossip and eat instead. I adored the female camaraderie and looked forward to the few short hours I spent each week in the company of my lady friends. We took turns meeting at somebody's house, and this afternoon we were meeting in the hotel parlor.

While the hotel was not richly appointed compared to establishments back east, it was very comfortable, and a veritable paradise considering the rough accommodations of Shoalwater Bay. Many of the furnishings had been shipped from San Francisco. Warm oriental rugs lined the hallways, and the parlor, which I considered the nicest room in the hotel, featured two velvet-padded settees, as well as a shelf that held the beginnings of a library.

Mrs. Frink was insistent that all men should read. I had been dubious at first but was astonished to find that the oystermen were quite voracious readers. The two most popular books were *The Gold-Seeker's Manual: Being a Practical and Instructive Guide to All Persons Emigrating to the Newly-Discovered Gold Regions of California*, and a book about a lady called *The Wide, Wide World*, by Miss Elizabeth Wetherell.

I had just finished setting out the tea when the ladies began to arrive.

"Hello, Jane!" they called out.

The ladies filed in—Mrs. Woodley, Mrs. Hosmer, Mrs. Staroselsky, and, of course, Mrs. Frink. We had invited Mrs. Dodd, the laundress, to our little gatherings, but she never came, nor did Millie.

We settled around the parlor.

"How are things at the store?" Mrs. Frink asked Mrs. Staroselsky.

"We finally got in those sewing needles I ordered," Mrs. Staroselsky replied with flashing eyes. "For some reason, barrels of whiskey have no problem finding their way to Shoalwater Bay, but there never seems to be room in the cargo hold for a small packet of sewing needles!"

We all laughed.

"Speaking of whiskey, you'll never guess what I witnessed the other morning," I said mysteriously.

"Oh, do tell us, Jane," Mrs. Woodley encouraged me.

"Well," I said to my captive audience. "Apparently the men were drinking rather late into the evening." I paused for effect. "And gambling."

This brought rolled eyes and clucking.

"In any event, one of the gentlemen, I believe his name is Mr. Whitney, gambled away all of his funds and was still quite desperate to play cards, so he gambled away his shirt."

"His shirt?" Mrs. Hosmer exclaimed.

"And his trousers," I added blandly.

Mrs. Hosmer's mouth opened in an *O* of shock.

"Which is how I came to see a man wearing a white chemise with a very nice length of lace at the hem wandering through town early the next morning," I finished.

The room burst into laughter.

"That was my good chemise!" Mrs. Woodley exclaimed in an indignant voice. "He must have stolen it off the line!"

"The least he could have done was pay you for it," Mrs. Frink said with a laugh.

Mrs. Hosmer began to speak, but her words were drowned out by a flurry of loud shouting from outside. The shouting grew louder and louder, escalating until it was a roar.

"Really," Mrs. Frink said. "Can't we have five minutes' peace and quiet?"

While the arrival of ladies on the bay had brought a civilizing influence on the whiskey-drinking men, I feared there were not nearly enough of us around to turn the tide of raucous and wild behavior. It was for this very reason that Mr. Frink required that all guests turn in their guns to be locked in the hotel safe.

"Excuse me," I said, and got up, walked to the front door, and flung it open.

Two men were wrestling in the mud of Front Street while another group watched and cheered them on.

"Gentlemen!" I shouted above the din. "If you do not cease your carousing, there will be no supper served at the hotel this evening."

The men abruptly stopped their shouting and looked at me with stricken faces.

"We are trying to have tea," I said in a firm voice.

The men nodded sheepishly.

"We sure are real sorry, Miss Peck," one of them said.

"You bet we are. We'll be right quiet from now on," another offered.

"Thank you," I said, and closed the door.

The ladies applauded when I returned to the parlor.

"Well done, Jane!" Mrs. Frink exclaimed.

Mrs. Staroselsky was laughing so hard she hiccuped. "I don't know what we'd do without you, Jane," she said, eyes watering.

I felt a flush of pride.

"These tarts are lovely, Jane," Mrs. Woodley said, eating her fourth one. "Although I probably shouldn't be eating so many sweets." She patted her plump waist. "My corset barely fits as it is!"

"I'd be happy to give you the receipt," I offered, pleased. I turned to Mrs. Hosmer. "How did the pie turn out?"

Mrs. Hosmer wrinkled her nose. "I'm afraid that I forgot to take it out and it got rather brown on top. But my husband said it was the best pie I had ever baked him!"

"Speaking of baking," Mrs. Staroselsky said, "has anyone given any thought to the Fourth of July festivities?"

"I suppose we could do something here in the hotel," Mrs. Frink said.

I shook my head. "Believe me, I think it's best if it's held outside, preferably far from anything that can burn down."

I had been in attendance for the previous Fourth of July celebration, which had been a wild, raucous party marked by a massive consumption of whiskey.

Mrs. Woodley chuckled. "I heard about last year's party, all right. Mr. Russell said it went on all night long!"

"And all morning," I added.

"Well then, Jane, would you consider coming up with some suggestions for the Fourth of July celebration?" Mrs. Frink asked.

"I'd be delighted to," I said.

"Wonderful! And be sure to let me know if there is anything I need to special-order," Mrs. Staroselsky said.

"Now, I understand we have some new arrivals. Ladies?"

"Mrs. Biddle and her daughter, Miss Biddle, of Philadelphia," Mrs. Hosmer said. "They're lovely!"

"Perhaps they'll join our sewing circle," Mrs. Woodley mused.

"I don't really think they'd enjoy the sewing circle," I said with hesitation.

"But I adore sewing! How could you forget, Jane?" a voice called behind me.

I winced, turning around slowly.

Sally Biddle stood there wearing a cashmere gown of soft sea green, cut close to the figure, with demi-sleeves. The collar was tied with a loose pink ribbon, and the outfit was topped off by a smart little cap with matching pink and green ribbons. The resulting ensemble gave the effect of a young lady out on a spring stroll. I had little doubt that it was the latest in Philadelphia fashion.

"Good afternoon, Mrs. Hosmer," Sally said with an incline of her head. "Mrs. Frink."

"How lovely to see you, Miss Biddle!" Mrs. Hosmer said in an excited voice. "Have you met Mrs. Woodley?"

Sally smiled at Mrs. Woodley. "How do you do?"

"Very nice to meet you," Mrs. Woodley said.

"And this is Mrs. Staroselsky," Mrs. Hosmer continued with the introductions. "She and her husband own—"

"Star's Dry Goods! You have a lovely store," Sally

said, flipping open a fan and fluttering it lazily.

"Thank you," Mrs. Staroselsky said. "And welcome to Shoalwater Bay!"

"You must join our sewing circle," Mrs. Hosmer said enthusiastically. "We have such fun!"

I held my breath. Surely Sally wouldn't take her up on the offer.

"I would simply *love* to come," Sally said, bringing the full force of her Philadelphia charm to bear. "Thank you so much for inviting me!"

"Wonderful!" Mrs. Staroselsky said.

"Wonderful," I echoed.

"I wouldn't miss it for the world," Sally said with a wicked little grin.

or,

A Room with a View

The hotel's rooms were quite cozy, and mine was no exception. It was warm and comfortable, and I didn't have to worry about waking up with some strange man in the bunk above me. Best of all, it had a perfect view of the bay.

I had accepted an invitation to dine at Chief Toke's lodge that evening and had left the running of the kitchen in Spaark's capable hands. I was trying to put my hair into some semblance of a style when there was a knock at the door.

It was Sally, and she was holding a beautiful gown in her arms.

"Is this your room?" Sally asked, stepping inside without an invitation.

"Yes," I said.

Sally scanned the room with sharp eyes. "Why, you have a view," she said, strolling to the window.

"May I help you?" I asked pointedly.

She took one last look at the bay and turned to me. "As a matter of fact, I expect you must."

"Excuse me?" I said, taken aback.

"How very naughty of you to deceive me, Jane," Sally replied spiritedly. "I wonder what Miss Hepplewhite would think about her favorite student telling a fib."

"What are you talking about?" I said.

"Why, Jane. You encouraged me to assume you were a paying guest, when in fact, Mrs. Frink has informed me that you are *employed* here." She gave a little laugh.

"Yes, I am the concierge, and I enjoy my job very much."

"That is good, because I need my frock pressed for tonight. I gave it to that Millie woman and she missed half the pleats!" Sally's eyes twinkled with delight. "Fortunately, you of all people will understand how high our standards are back in Philadelphia."

With a flourish, Sally tossed her gown at me and sauntered out of the room.

The sun was sinking into the bay, turning the landscape a glorious shade of gold. I followed the path that led from Mr. Russell's cabin down to the stream where Father Joseph lived, and on to the Chinook village.

Father Joseph, a French Catholic missionary, had come to Shoalwater Bay on the same ship as I had. He was trying to convert the Chinooks and had not been very successful. Although he did have one recent convert—Auntie Lilly, an older Chinook lady.

Auntie Lilly had been married to a Hudson's Bay Company man, but she had been abandoned by him when he returned to England on a ship and neglected to tell her he was going. For her part, Auntie Lilly did not seem all that upset that her English husband was gone, as it was well known that he had not been a particularly kind man.

These days Auntie Lilly spent a great deal of time with Father Joseph, and not just listening to his sermons. She cooked his meals, bargained for his supplies, and even cajoled some of the Chinook children to attend services. They had become good companions to each other in their own way.

I found Auntie Lilly at the stream washing what appeared to be one of Father Joseph's wool robes. The Chinooks were great believers in bathing, and cleanliness in general, and I had hoped more than once that this habit would rub off on the local pioneer men, who thought nothing of wearing the same pair of trousers for weeks on end.

"It certainly is very kind of you to do Father Joseph's washing for him," I said.

She clucked her tongue, slapping his robe in the

cool stream. Gray streaked her hair, giving it a silvery tint. "Who else will do it if I do not?"

"Perhaps the angels?" I said wryly.

Auntie Lilly guffawed. "Angels? They will run from these robes."

I laughed.

The owner of the filthy robes was sitting outside a rustic chapel, reading a Bible.

"Hello, Father Joseph," I called.

A smile wreathed his lips. "Mademoiselle! What brings you here?"

"I'm going to Chief Toke's lodge for supper," I said. "How are you?"

"*Très bien, merci.* Auntie Lilly has been encouraging the children to go to church, you see. I think they are all very much enjoying my sermons! Auntie Lilly has been so helpful!" Father Joseph enthused.

"Yes," I teased. "I noticed that she was very helpfully doing your laundry."

He blushed so brightly that even his bald head turned red.

"I best be going," I said, and headed on.

Farther down the trail, I saw a plump, white-bearded, bespectacled man sitting on a log, studying a small book. It was Mr. Swan, another longtime resident of Shoalwater Bay and my business partner.

"Why, hello, my dear!" Mr. Swan declared. "Where are you off to on this fine evening?"

"To Chief Toke's lodge. For supper."

"Capital! Then I shall join you, as I am going there myself! I do so look forward to a good Chinook feast!"

As we strolled along Mr. Swan waved his ever present diary. "Chief Toke is having a new canoe made, and he promised to show it to me after supper. I have been making notes on its construction. It is fascinating!"

Mr. Swan was something of an amateur anthropologist, or "adventurer" as he liked to call himself, and he spent much of his time studying the local flora and fauna, as well as the Chinook Indians. Known as one of the original American settlers on Shoalwater Bay, he'd arrived here several years ago from Boston. In fact, he still had a wife and two daughters back there, although he never spoke of them. Mr. Swan presently resided in Mr. Russell's cabin.

"Squire!" a voice called.

As there was no formal local government, Mr. Swan currently acted as the unofficial judge in local disputes, and the men had taken to calling him squire.

Red Charley came stomping up to us, dragging a thin man by the arm. "Me and Joe here are having a dispute." Red Charley grinned at me, revealing his yellow teeth. "Howdy, Miss Peck."

"Good evening, Mr. Charley," I said.

"Explain the situation, my good man," Mr. Swan said.

Red Charley's face grew annoyed. "See, I gave Joe here a barrel of whiskey on credit, and he went and drank it, and now I want my money to buy me a new roof, and he won't give it to me!"

"Is this true? Did he give it to you on credit?" Mr. Swan asked.

The man scratched his head sheepishly. "He did, but he didn't say *when* I had to pay 'im back. And I can't pay 'im now. I'm plumb broke!"

"Then you shouldn'ta drank that whiskey!" Red Charley muttered.

"Hmmm," Mr. Swan said, rubbing his chin thoughtfully. "I believe I have a solution."

The two men held their breath for his verdict.

"As you are in need of a new roof," he said, looking at Red Charley, "and you have no funds," he said to Joe, "why don't you build a new roof for Charley, Joe? In return, he shall forgive your debt."

The men regarded each other and then slowly shook their heads in agreement.

"I reckon that would be okay," Red Charley said, almost reluctantly. "But that's the last time I give you any whiskey on credit!"

"Capital!" Mr. Swan said, and slapped both men on their backs. "Now, I'm afraid that we must move along, as I am escorting Miss Peck to supper."

"O' course," Red Charley said, tipping his hat. "Thankee, Squire."

Mr. Swan paused, looking back. "Charley, would you be so kind as to lend me some whiskey? I'm afraid I'm rather light for coins at the moment."

"Your credit's always good with me, Squire!" Red Charley said.

I shook my head. Mr. Swan shared the men of Shoalwater Bay's affection for drinking too much whiskey. Still, in spite of this failing, he was greatly respected by all. He had helped more than one man secure oyster beds and negotiate for help from the Chinooks.

Ahead of us in the distance loomed a collection of large buildings. It was the Chinook village. The Chinooks built massive lodges of cedar that were so big that they had the capacity to house several families in comfort.

We entered Chief Toke's lodge by slipping through an opening near the ground. Fire pits lined the center of the lodge, and cedar planks that could be shifted served as the roof, allowing smoke to escape. Huge bunk-like structures, platforms really, were built along the interior walls and housed entire families. The Chinooks lived in perfect luxury compared to the settlers in their tiny cabins. I had spent many a happy evening in this lodge, and I immediately felt at home.

"Well, if it isn't Miss Peck!" a voice cried, and I turned to see M'Carty and his wife sitting with Chief Toke on a high platform along with Keer-ukso. Mr. Russell was there as well, I noticed, and Sootie and Katy were giggling away in a corner with their dolls.

M'Carty and Mr. Russell had been the first settlers

to arrive on the bay, and the two were fast friends. M'Carty had helped to establish the territory's now thriving oyster business and owned a schooner that he hired out to ferry the oysters to San Francisco. He had married Cocumb, who was one of Chief Toke's daughters. They made a handsome couple.

"Boston Jane," Cocumb said with a warm smile. She and I had become good friends during my time on the bay.

"*Kahta mika?*" she asked. *How are you?*

"*Kloshe kahkwa,*" I replied. *Very well.*

Cocumb smiled approvingly. "Your Jargon is coming along well."

The Jargon was the local trading language, and it consisted mainly of Chinook, with some French and English words as well.

Katy and Sootie rushed over to me.

"Boston Jane," Katy said. "You must come and help us with our dolls!"

Cocumb smiled and smoothed back Katy's hair. "After supper, *tenas klootchman.*"

We all sat down and bowls of food were passed around. I took some *camas*, a Chinook specialty, and some roasted salmon.

I had just taken a bite of the salmon when Mr. Russell announced without preamble, "Baldt's back."

I choked. "When?"

Mr. Russell spit. "This morning."

William's return was not good news. My former

betrothed now worked for the governor as an Indian agent, and he did not look upon the Chinooks favorably. There was a moment of worried silence.

"Saw him in town with that new feller from Philadelphia," Mr. Russell finally said.

"Mr. Biddle?" I asked, dumbfounded.

"Yep." Mr. Russell nodded. "They were having themselves a real conversation. All businesslike, if you know what I mean."

Of course! How could I have not thought of it myself? It explained why Mr. Biddle was here on Shoalwater Bay, the most unlikely of places. William had known Mr. Biddle back in Philadelphia. They had traveled in the same circles. No doubt William had written him about the prospects for land speculation in the territory.

"It doesn't matter whether he's back or not," Cocumb said. "My father still isn't interested in that reservation treaty he's selling." She glanced at Chief Toke, who gave a small nod.

Mr. Russell grunted. "They might not even bother asking."

"Mr. Russell," I said, "they would not dare, would they? Things have been quite peaceful."

And this was true. The settlers and Indians lived together agreeably. In fact, the settlers would have been unable to run their oyster businesses without the Indians. They depended on them for help in harvesting the oysters.

Keer-ukso leaned over. "Boston Jane is right," he said with a grin. "All these new people are good. There will be jobs and more money for us!"

With the recent influx of pioneers on the bay, the Chinook found their labor in great demand.

"Yes," Mr. Swan said enthusiastically. "Our little community is growing by leaps and bounds. And I firmly believe that our new arrivals will see that they can profit by developing a good relationship with you." He paused, looking around. "Speaking of profit, anyone care for a friendly wager?"

"Mr. Swan!" I hissed. Gambling had gotten Mr. Swan into trouble in the past.

"Just one game, dear girl. To win back what I lost last week!"

I looked across at Cocumb, who shook her head in silent communion.

Cocumb turned to her husband, a shadow of worry in her eyes. "What if Mr. Russell's right?"

"Don't you worry none, *nayka klootchman*." M'Carty hugged her to him and laughed heartily. "Nothing's gonna happen as long as I have breath in this body of mine. I take care of my own."

Mr. Russell belched.

When I returned to the hotel, Mr. Frink was carrying one of Sally's trunks down the hall. I followed him as he shouldered it . . . into *my room*! Sally was standing in the middle of the space, her possessions arrayed everywhere. A pile of her trunks rested in the corner where my desk had once been. Mrs. Frink was standing next to her.

"You can put it right there," Sally said to Mr. Frink. He put it down and straightened, rubbing his shoulder.

Sally turned and noticed me standing in the doorway.

"Oh, Jane darling," she said. "I was just telling Mrs. Frink how sweet you were to suggest that we change rooms. You're such a dear friend to remember that I have trouble sleeping unless there is a good cross breeze. The air does seem better in this room."

My mouth dropped open so wide, I'm surprised a bird didn't fly into it.

"That's why our Jane is the best concierge on the bay!" Mrs. Frink gushed.

"She certainly is," Sally agreed with a smile.

or,

Husband Material

The next morning, after my chores were finished, I decided to go over to my claim to see how my house was coming along, and with particular interest now that I had been kicked out of my room.

Not that anyone knew what had really happened. Mrs. Frink thought Sally was perfectly charming.

"Such a nice young lady. And so thoughtful," Mrs. Frink said. "Do you know that she said this is one of the nicest hotels she's ever stayed at! I was so touched."

As I walked along the windswept shore, the salty breeze tangling my hair, I pondered news more worrisome than Sally Biddle.

William was back on Shoalwater Bay, no doubt stirring up trouble.

These thoughts of my father's old apprentice

brought a longing for Papa so deep, I could barely breathe. Papa had died of consumption after I left to come west to marry William. My dear, sweet father who used to have me sit on sailors' bellies while he set their broken legs.

"A man won't scream so much if a little girl's sitting on his belly, Janey," he liked to say with a wink.

Papa had not believed that William was worthy of me, but he had not lived to learn that I had discovered as much. I had been preparing to return home when I received word of my father's death. It still broke my heart to think that Papa had died all alone, and all because I had foolishly followed William out west.

I was smitten by William at first glance. With his bright blond hair and handsome gray eyes, William had appeared to be an angel fallen to earth, and I had done everything in my young way to please him, down to wearing only green dresses, which he claimed suited me. It was he who had encouraged me to enter Miss Hepplewhite's, and he who had counseled me on the importance of fitting in with other girls, like Sally.

He took advantage of my girlhood infatuation, coaxing me with love letters to join him on Shoalwater Bay, against my father's better judgment. I learned too late that William had sent me a proposal of marriage only because a married man could claim twice as much land as an unmarried man. When my ship was delayed, William, fearing that he would lose out on his precious land, took an Indian wife.

It saddened me to think that Papa had been right after all. But I also liked to think that Papa would have been proud of how well his wild, red-haired daughter had survived.

As I neared my claim, I felt my heart ease at the sight of my land. It had been a gift to me from Jehu. Only white men were allowed to have claims in Washington Territory. In order to get around this little problem, Jehu had simply written "J. Peck" on my paperwork, and no one was the wiser.

Up on the grassy hill, I saw evidence that Jehu and Keer-ukso had been hard at work. Part of the roof was up, and various tools and supplies were scattered about. But no one was in sight.

"Jehu!" I called.

"Over here, Boston Jane," I heard Keer-ukso shout from somewhere behind the house.

I made my way toward a shelter of trees, where Keer-ukso stood staring down at the ground and shaking his head.

"Boston Jane, tell Jehu that the hole is big enough and to come help finish roof," Keer-ukso said.

I peered down into the deep hole to see Jehu, covered head to toe in mud, digging away.

"What are you doing down there?" I asked.

He grinned up at me. "Digging you a privy!"

I reddened.

Keer-ukso clucked his tongue. "It's deep enough. Come help with roof."

Jehu rubbed a dirty forearm across his face, leaving a brown smear. "I reckon you're right. What do you think, Jane?" he teased.

"It's quite adequate," I said primly.

Jehu looked up to Keer-ukso. "Here, give me a hand up."

We three walked back to my house, and then I stood with Keer-ukso while Jehu went down to the stream to wash off.

Keer-ukso patted me on the arm. "Jehu, he is crazy to dig that hole."

"Would you dig a hole for Spaark?"

"*Nowitka,*" he said, his expression serious. *Nowitka* meant certainly. A mischievous gleam entered his eye. "But I would have Jehu do the digging!"

I laughed.

"What's so funny?" Jehu asked.

Jehu stood at the edge of the clearing, his skin slick with a fine sheen of water. He looked so handsome standing there, his black curly hair brushing the nape of his neck, his face tanned from years at sea. My heart gave a little flip just looking at him.

"I am telling Boston Jane that you have no sense," Keer-ukso said.

But Jehu was barely listening to him. He was staring at me with those beautiful blue eyes of his, and I blushed under his knowing gaze, hastily pushing a rather vexing lock of hair off my forehead. Jehu caught my eye and gave me a little wink.

"Have time for a cup of coffee?" he asked, his voice husky, the tilt of his head rakish as any self-respecting pirate's.

"I need to get back to help organize supper."

"Not so fast, Miss Peck," Jehu teased, easily grabbing my hand in his warm larger one and tugging me in the direction of his house. "I reckon you can spare a minute for the man who dug your privy."

Keer-ukso looked up at the sky in mock irritation. "No, do not ask *me*, best friend and business partner, if *I* want coffee?"

Jehu looked back at Keer-ukso and grinned. "Go on and get started. I'll bring you some on the roof in a moment."

Keer-ukso scoffed.

Jehu had taken a claim on a piece of land bordering mine, and on it stood a small, sturdy cabin. It was tidy and smelled good, like him. I took a seat at the table— a beautiful piece of furniture, the top hewn from a single piece of cedar. Jehu was a marvelous carpenter, having worked for so many years on ships.

He gently pushed a curl off my forehead and tucked it behind my ear, brushing his lips against my cheek. I leaned into him, the stress of hearing news of William Baldt melting away in the face of Jehu's easy company.

"Let me get that coffee," he murmured.

I felt a warm tingle in my belly as I surreptitiously watched him add three sugars and a careful pour of milk to one mug. It was exactly the way I liked it.

Miss Hepplewhite would have been appalled to see Jehu do the pouring. She believed it was a lady's duty to entertain a gentleman, and pouring tea and coffee was held in particularly high esteem. But as Jehu handed me the mug and I took my first sweet, perfect sip, I knew that Miss Hepplewhite had been most mistaken. Truly, there was nothing better this side of heaven than having Jehu Scudder pour my coffee.

"When do you think the house will be finished?" I asked.

"I reckon we can have you in by the Fourth of July."

"Marvelous!" I said.

"When we have the lumber mill up and running, things will be a lot easier." He leaned forward, his eyes intent. "I tell you, Jane, this lumber mill is going to make a fortune. The way me and Keer-ukso have it figured, we have good relations with most of the settlers, and people are starting to clear their land. Whoever gets a mill up first will get the best contracts, and we aim for it to be us.

"All we need now is some capital. Sooner or later, some prospector is going to turn up with a pocketful of gold, and I'll be just the man to invest in," he said.

Jehu had been a successful sea captain, but he had given up the sea to remain here on Shoalwater Bay and

60

make a life with me. What if he couldn't succeed in this dream? I would do anything I could to make his new venture successful, but unfortunately I had no connections in such matters, nor did I have funds. Several months before, I had written our family solicitor in Philadelphia requesting him to send me the details of my inheritance from my father, but I had heard no reply as yet. I actually had no idea how much money there was from the sale of our house on Walnut Street, although I feared it would never be enough to help Jehu.

"Keer-ukso and I will be rich men one day, mark my words," he said with a touch of rakish confidence. One black curl flopped across his forehead.

And then Jehu leaned across the table and kissed me, a kiss sweeter than the very sugar in my coffee. It tasted like hope and the future all wrapped up together in one long heartbeat.

"Oh Jehu," I said, swallowing hard. "I just know you'll succeed."

"But only if I get back to work." He tweaked my nose. "Now I best go take Keer-ukso some coffee before he gets irritable."

"Keer-ukso never gets irritable," I said.

"You haven't seen him without his coffee."

I punched him in the arm and he chuckled.

Mrs. Frink was waiting for me in the kitchen when I returned to the hotel. And she was looking decidedly ruffled.

"Jane," she said, working at sounding calm, "there's a gentleman in the parlor who would like to speak to you."

"Really?" I asked. "Did he give his name?"

Mrs. Frink cast a wary glance over her shoulder and lowered her voice a notch. "No."

As I rounded the corner, an incredibly gamy scent hit my nose. And then I saw the enormous bundle of fur sitting on the parlor's best settee.

"Hairy Bill!" I exclaimed in delight.

"Miss Jane," he said with a respectful tip of his head.

Hairy Bill was one of Shoalwater Bay's most notorious men. An accomplished thief, he had been run off the bay the previous fall for stealing. He had gotten his unusual name from the massive cape of animal pelts that he wore everywhere.

"How are you, Mr. Hairy?" I asked.

He removed a rifle from the folds of his furry cape and cackled. "Reckon you didn't think you'd ever see this again!"

I must admit that I was astonished. I *had* never expected to see that rifle again. M'Carty had lent it to Jehu, but Hairy Bill had disappeared with it following a chance encounter. Although he had left an I.O.U., I recalled.

"Thank you," I said, taking the rifle from him. "I'm sure M'Carty will be happy to have this back."

He nodded. "I always settle my debts."

"Are you supposed to be in town?" I asked carefully.

"I reckon not," he said, and sniffed the air. "That sure does smell good."

"Come into the kitchen," I said with a good-natured laugh.

I set out several serving dishes in front of him—roast chicken, hard-boiled eggs, leftover baked potatoes from the previous night's supper, oyster pie, fresh milk, and some biscuits from breakfast. It was a feast large enough for several men.

Hairy Bill attacked the food as if he hadn't had a decent meal in months. In no time at all he had eaten every scrap in sight, and with a satisfied expression on his face, he sat back and belched.

"'Scuse me," he said. "That was mighty tasty. You sure are a real good cook, Miss Jane." He leaned back in his chair. "So you work here now?"

"I do," I said. "And I have a room upstairs."

"Sure is a nice place," he said, an edge of longing to his voice.

"Yes, it is," I agreed.

"And that Jehu feller, how's he?" he asked with a knowing look.

"Jehu is very well. Thank you for asking." I blushed.

Hairy Bill chuckled. "He'll make a good husband, eh?"

I poured us each a cup of tea. "Now you've heard all

about me. Where have you been?" I asked.

"Jest about everywhere in the territory, I reckon," he said.

"Weren't you going to try and woo your wife back?" I asked.

When I had met Mr. Hairy late this past fall, he had expressed his great desire to win back the love of his wife, who had kicked him out. Clearly I had hit a raw nerve, for the man's face fell and tears welled in his eyes.

"Well, I paid a preacher feller to write her a letter and sent it, but didn't hear from her, so I went back to see her," he mumbled.

"And what happened?"

Fat tears began to slip down his cheeks. He wiped at his eyes with a mangy scrap of fur.

"Oh, please, Mr. Hairy," I beseeched him. "Don't cry. Here, use my handkerchief," I said, passing him my own white lace one.

He blew into it and wailed, "When I got there, there was another feller living in my house!"

"So what did you do?" I asked.

"Nothing I could do," he said with a sad sigh. "You can't make another person love you. Why, that would be like asking a pig to fly. A person's gotta come to you on their own."

I considered Jehu, and our long courtship, and thought of how far we had come. "I suppose you're right."

There was a long pause while we both considered his sad tale.

"Jane," he said.

"What?"

"You know I'm pulling your leg, doncha?"

"What?" I exclaimed.

He guffawed. "Jane, you sure are a sweet girl and all, but you gotta wise up! How'm I gonna walk all the way to Richmond? I've been in Astoria the whole time. Finally ran out of whiskey money."

"Jehu told me not to believe you!" I said.

"Yep, you've got a good man all right. I'd hang on to him if'n I was you." He yawned widely and heaved himself up, tugging his furry cape around his shoulders. "I reckon I better be moving on now. Thanks for lunch, Miss Jane."

"Why don't you stay here for a night or two?" I asked impulsively. Really, thief or not, this man had once saved Jehu's life, and he had obviously been having a very hard time of it lately.

"I don't have that kind of money, Miss Peck," he said.

"You can stay in the storage room. It's dry and we can fix up a bed for you. Maybe you can lend a hand around here in return."

"Well that's mighty kind of you, Miss Jane," he said.

"Just don't . . . *borrow* anything," I warned.

"You've got my word of honor," Hairy Bill promised

in a sincere voice. "I'm a reformed man."

I had no sooner settled Hairy Bill than I heard someone ring the bell at the desk. A man was standing with his back turned to me, looking out the curtained parlor window.

"May I help you?" I asked.

"Jane," said my former betrothed.

He looked much the same as when I had last seen him. If anything, he looked better, even more handsome.

"Happy to see me?" William drawled.

"Not particularly," I said. "I already knew you were in town."

"My, but you do keep track of my movements. Could it be that you still have some affection for me?"

"Not likely," I snapped. "What do you want?"

"I should think that would be apparent enough," he said. "I'd like a room."

"A room? Here?"

"This is a hotel, is it not?" William scrutinized my blue dress. "I see you have persisted in spurning my advice."

Green suits you, Jane. You should always wear green.

"I prefer blue," I said. "So tell me, Dr. Baldt, what are you doing these days? Planning to round up the local Indians and put them on a reservation?"

"Actually, I'm here on a private matter," he informed me in an important tone. "Business."

I felt relief wash over me at the revelation that he was not here to endanger the Chinooks. Still, what was he up to?

"I understand you've been spending quite a bit of time with Mr. Biddle," I said. "How interesting. Did you lure him out here with lies as you did me?"

"Jane, Jane," William said as if I were a tiresome child. "It was certainly fortuitous that we did not marry. You would not have made a suitable wife."

"And where is your wife?" I shot back.

"I sent her back to her tribe."

"That's very romantic," I said in a sarcastic voice.

"For your information," he said coolly, "she was homesick. And what would you know about romance anyway?"

I felt a flush burn through me.

"I know quite a bit. In fact, I'll have you know that I'm engaged to be married." I immediately bit my lip. I couldn't believe I'd just said that!

William looked stung even though *he'd* been the one to throw me over. He regained his equilibrium quickly.

"Is that a fact?" he asked. "To whom?"

I swallowed and blustered on. "Mr. Jehu Scudder."

"Ah, yes. The sailor with the scar." He contemplated this for a moment. "At least he's a suitable husband for someone who's turned out the way you have."

"What's that supposed to mean?"

"Simply that your father would be disappointed

in this turn of events."

"My father would be proud of me! And besides, he never wanted me to marry you in the first place!"

"You've never learned not to contradict people who know better." He shook his head as if he couldn't be bothered. "I'll come back when you've regained your composure."

"Go jump in the bay!" I shouted.

I stared at his departing back, furious at myself for letting him bait me into saying that I was engaged to Jehu. But then again, I thought, why shouldn't I? Jehu and I were going to spend the future together, weren't we? Everyone assumed we were getting married, even Hairy Bill. Why, he was building me a house and digging me a privy, for heaven's sakes! A man would not dig a privy for a woman he did not care for, I knew that much.

But a tiny thought nagged at me. Jehu had never actually *asked* me to marry him. Even horrible William had had the decency to offer me a proper proposal of marriage, and Keer-ukso and Red Charley proposed to me every other day.

Only Jehu, the man who held my heart, had never actually said the simple words I longed to hear, the ones I heard in my head even now.

Jane, will you be my wife?

CHAPTER SIX

or,

Pies

I had spent the better part of the next morning making certain that the hotel was in good order, and my duties seemed endless. I checked with Millie the schedule of rooms to be cleaned. I drew up an order for Star's. I negotiated a payment plan with an oysterman. I managed to find a spare trouser button for one of our male guests, as well as a hat pin for Mrs. Biddle.

Now, as I stole a quiet moment in the kitchen after the rush and clatter of breakfast, the back door banged open. Jehu sauntered in and put a jar on the table.

"What's that?" I asked.

"Molasses." He was looking pleased with himself.

"Why would I want a jar of molasses?" I burst out.

Jehu's smile slipped. "So you can make pies, of course."

"Is that all I'm good for?" I asked wildly. "Baking pies?"

Jehu looked behind him nervously. "I best be going. There's a ship coming in that I need to help unload."

And he was gone.

I stood there staring at the door as it banged against the frame like a portent of doom. The door to the kitchen bounced open and I started, expecting to see Jehu standing there.

It was Spaark carrying a basket.

"I just saw Jehu," she said. "Going that way."

I took a deep, calming breath. What had come over me?

She looked quizzically at the molasses on the table. "I thought you told me to buy molasses."

"Jehu brought that."

Her eyes were shiny with excitement.

"Why are you so happy?" I asked.

"Keer-ukso," she said. "He said when the mill is up he will be a rich man, and then can trade with my father and I will be his wife!"

"Oh," I said, feeling unaccountably sorry for myself. "That's wonderful."

She looked at me quizzically. "What's wrong, Boston Jane? You like Keer-ukso, yes?"

I looked down, shamefaced. Who was I to ruin her happiness?

"Boston Jane," she said, laying a gentle hand on my arm.

"It's not that," I said, swallowing hard. "It's Jehu."

"Jehu?"

I looked out the kitchen window. "I want to marry him."

"But your father is dead. He doesn't need money to trade with your father. You can get married tomorrow if you want. You are lucky!"

"That's not it," I said. "It's not the Boston custom for the man to trade with a father to get a wife. If anything, it's the opposite. The woman brings a dowry and—" I stopped myself, shaking my head. "That's not it at all."

"What is it then?"

"Jehu hasn't asked me to marry him."

Spaark looked perplexed. "Then why don't you ask him to marry you?"

I shook my head. "That just isn't how it's done."

She nodded as if considering this problem. Then her eyes brightened. "Maybe you can still do it the Chinook way. It does not have to be your father, it can be someone who is like a father. Like Mr. Swan! You have Jehu pay Mr. Swan!"

"He'd just gamble it away!"

Spaark giggled. "Or spend it on Red Charley's whiskey!"

We both laughed.

"I see your problem," she said finally. "You must trust your friends. And your friends tell you not to worry. Jehu will marry you, Boston Jane."

As I looked into her kind eyes, I couldn't help thinking:

But I still want him to ask *me!*

In the end, I used the molasses Jehu had given me to make pies.

As usual we were to have a full house for supper. The evening's menu included oyster soup, oyster tarts, fried oysters, and mashed potatoes, as well as my molasses pies cooling on the windowsill.

Oysters were a delicacy most places, but here on the bay they were a staple. We served them many different ways to keep them interesting—stewed, fried, broiled, fricasseed, deviled, curried, steamed, au gratin, pickled, as fritters, in pies, in omelets, in tarts, in soup, and sometimes as a sauce. But by far the most popular method of eating oysters was raw in whiskey, although Mrs. Frink made the men go to the taverns for that.

I personally hated oysters. They resembled fat slugs.

Even though the Frink Hotel catered to all manner of men, I worried that the sight of Hairy Bill would ruin the appetites of more than one of our guests. Not to mention, he wasn't supposed to be on the bay to begin with. So I made a point of delivering a tray to Hairy Bill's room before supper.

"Don't worry, Miss Jane," Hairy Bill said, as he happily dug into the food. "I got everything I want right here. Don't see no reason to leave."

That was, of course, what I was starting to fear.

William, I knew, would be attending supper, and despite my good intentions to the contrary, I took great pains with my appearance, selecting my best dress—a dress made of lovely gold silk that I had sewn myself from a pattern I recalled seeing in Philadelphia. It set off my red hair and suited me perfectly. What was it about him that made me want to prove myself again and again? After all this time, why did I care about his opinion?

Once downstairs, I left Mrs. Frink to greet the arriving guests and poked my head into the kitchen to check on the meal. As usual everything was running smoothly thanks to Spaark and Millie.

"Where's Willard?" I asked, glancing around the kitchen. Willard was supposed to help Millie with the serving and clearing.

Spaark rolled her eyes.

"Haven't seen him since this morning," Millie admitted. "He disappeared after I told him to scrub out the milk urn."

"That boy is useless." I slipped on my apron and grabbed a tray of biscuits. "Well, it appears that I shall be helping you this evening, Millie."

The guests were already seated and conversation filled the room. All the tables were jammed elbow to elbow. At one end of the head table sat Mr. and Mrs.

Frink, Mr. Swan, the Hosmers, and Father Joseph, and at the other end, where I was to sit, were Mr. and Mrs. Biddle, Sally, and William. William had taken the seat next to Mr. Biddle, and the two men were looking very chummy. It was so strange to see them all together— it was almost as if Philadelphia had been transplanted to Shoalwater Bay!

Sally caught my eye and gave me a knowing look. It was clear who had arranged the seating. She was wearing a beautiful evening gown of icy silver, no doubt another of the very latest styles from *Godey's Lady's Book*. I suddenly felt like a scullery maid in my simple silk dress.

Mrs. Biddle sat opposite me, wearing a grand frock made of heavy brocade satin and a rather annoyed expression, as if she still weren't quite sure how she had found herself there.

"It is a pleasure to see you again, Mrs. Biddle," I said.

Mrs. Biddle merely fixed a scornful eye on my apron. "Do ladies not dress for supper here?"

William leaned over to Mrs. Biddle and smiled. "I assure you, Mrs. Biddle, that there are many here who are endeavoring to bring civilization to these wild shores."

Mrs. Biddle gave an approving little nod and said, "I should hope so. Mr. and Mrs. Frink assured me that this was a respectable establishment. I should hate to have to take our business elsewhere!"

Millie, who was serving the soup, met my eyes and we shared a little smirk. Where exactly did she plan to take her business? Mr. Russell's cabin?

"Oyster soup again?" Mrs. Biddle asked in a disagreeable voice. "I had oysters for supper last night, as well as for lunch today!"

"Oysters are our specialty, Mrs. Biddle," I explained. "You might even say that they are the blood of this town."

"Speaking of this town, I have an announcement to make," William said, brandishing an official-looking letter. "I bring word from the territorial government that there are to be local elections."

"Elections? What a marvelous idea!" Mrs. Frink said. She looked fetching in her soft brown dress, with her lovely hair pulled back in a simple knot. "For what positions?"

"For constable and justice of the peace, as well as for a representative to the legislature," William said.

"Why we need such legalities is quite beyond me. We are doing very well managing our own affairs," Mr. Swan said a little huffily.

Mrs. Frink rolled her eyes at this.

"I think it's a fine idea to have elections," I said. "Actually, you'd make a wonderful justice of the peace, Mr. Swan."

"Me?" Mr. Swan said, brightening. "Hadn't thought

of it myself, but why not?"

"You would be the perfect choice, Mr. Swan," Mrs. Frink said graciously. "I don't know how Mr. Frink and I would have been able to build the hotel without your guidance in local matters." She turned to the table and confided, "He was invaluable."

"And Mr. Swan helped us with our claim," Mrs. Hosmer said.

"Monsieur Swan helped secure a cask of fine wine for communion," Father Joseph added.

Mr. Swan reddened under the praise. "I was happy to be of assistance."

"Have you any experience in governing?" Mr. Biddle asked.

"Not exactly," Mr. Swan stuttered. "But I have served as judge in this part of the territory in an . . . ahem . . . unofficial capacity."

Mr. Biddle looked unimpressed. "Speaking of letters, did you say your name was Swan?"

Mr. Swan drew himself up proudly. "James G. Swan, at your service, sir."

"Humph," Mr. Biddle said, and fished in the pocket of his dinner jacket, extracting a thin letter. "The captain of a passing ship from Boston gave this to me to give to you." He held out the letter.

The letter was addressed to "James G. Swan, at Shoalwater Bay" in a feminine hand, the script cursive and flowing. Mr. Swan looked at the letter for a long moment and then reluctantly took it, his hand shaking slightly.

"Thank you," Mr. Swan said formally, and secreted the letter into his coat pocket.

"Who do you suppose shall run for constable?" Father Joseph asked.

Mr. Frink, who was normally quiet, chuckled. "Wouldn't be a speck of disorder if Jane was in charge of things round these parts!"

Mrs. Biddle looked appalled. "You are most certainly joking, sir."

"Our Jane here's a fine shot with a rifle," he said. "Apprehended a thief not too long ago."

Mrs. Hosmer turned to me, a nervous look on her face. "You're not serious, are you, Miss Peck? About becoming the constable? That sounds terribly dangerous."

I leaned over and whispered in her ear. "I assure you I have no ambition to be constable. But Mr. Frink is right. I am a good shot."

"Perhaps M'Carty could be constable?" Mr. Swan suggested. "After Mr. Russell, he knows the territory best and has been here the longest."

"He's married to that old chief's daughter," William commented, his voice thick with disapproval.

"Cocumb is a lovely lady," I said.

"She may be a lovely woman, but she is hardly a lady," William said. "She's a savage."

"I'll thank you not to insult my friend like that," I said between gritted teeth.

"Perhaps she is the exception that proves the rule, but I shouldn't like anyone who is our constable to be married to a savage," he said.

All talk at the table had ceased, and nine pairs of curious eyes regarded William and me.

Mr. Swan said hastily, "Ahem, so tell me, William, what brings you back to the bay? And is there money in it?" He laughed, a little too loudly.

William took a long sip of water, his blond hair glowing in the light of the candles. "I am surveying land," he said in a cool voice. "Apparently a number of fraudulent claims have been filed."

His eyes met mine across the table for a long moment, and I suddenly remembered the blond figure walking across my claim the day Sally had arrived.

William gave a cold little smile, and a shiver of unease ran through me.

I excused myself to check on progress in the kitchen. Millie was already loading her tray with bowls of mashed potatoes and platters of fried oysters.

"I tell you one thing," Millie said, all business now, snatching up a tray of chicken, "I am going to torture young Willard if he doesn't turn up in time to scrub the dishes."

"Why don't you take that out and I'll check his

regular haunts," I said.

I opened the back door of the kitchen and looked around.

"Willard!" I called.

There was a rush of movement and a loud clatter, the sound of barrels being knocked over. Someone cursed. The voice was too deep to be Willard's.

I peered into the darkness.

Two figures hovered over barrels containing various supplies that had been delivered by a late-arriving schooner that afternoon. I had neglected to have Mr. Frink move them into the storage room.

"Excuse me," I called. "May I help you?"

The men stumbled forward. I could smell the whiskey on their breath from where I stood.

One wore a red cap and was so tall and skinny that he resembled a scarecrow. The other fellow had a shiny gold front tooth and a bald head. I didn't recognize either one of them. They were, no doubt, recent arrivals, and of very poor character as well.

They stared at me with their beady, red-rimmed eyes for a long moment and then stumbled off into the darkness.

"How peculiar," I said to myself.

When I returned to my table, the topic of conversation had changed.

"So, William," Mr. Biddle was saying, "I liked the

plot of land you showed me yesterday, but what about the other land you wrote me of? There were several locations that sounded promising."

So my instincts had been correct, after all! William *had* written to Mr. Biddle.

"Of course," William said. "I thought we would survey that tomorrow."

"What piece of land did you show Mr. Biddle?" I asked.

William's eyes slid to mine. "Near the Chinook village. It is very well situated as a portage for timber."

"Near savages?" Mrs. Biddle gasped. "There are tepee villages nearby?" Her voice rose an octave. "I thought you said this area was perfectly safe!"

"Now, my dear," Mr. Biddle began.

"Savages!" Mrs. Biddle said again, and then whipped out her fan, waving frantically, patting her chest. "They'll kill us. And eat us. I've read the news reports! I know what horrible animals they are!"

"Mrs. Biddle," I said with a light laugh. "They're nothing of the sort—"

William interrupted me as if I hadn't even spoken. "I assure you, Mr. and Mrs. Biddle, that it is only a temporary concern. It is the stated intention of Governor Stevens to move these Indians to a reservation."

Always in the past, William had been one to foment poor relations with the Chinooks. And always in the past, he had failed to persuade anyone in our small community of his wisdom in this matter. I felt confident any new attempt would fail as well. That is, until Mr. Biddle turned to William and said, "That seems a very sensible idea, William."

"It isn't a sensible idea at all, Mr. Biddle," I said.

Mr. Biddle looked at me sharply.

Father Joseph echoed my sentiment. "This is their home."

To my surprise, it was Mr. Hosmer who said, "But, Father, how can you hope to civilize these poor souls if they are permitted to continue in their wild ways?"

Before Father Joseph could answer, I leaped in. "Please believe me when I say that the Chinooks who live here are the finest neighbors one could hope for."

"You give your opinions very freely, *young lady*." Mr. Biddle made a decidedly disapproving sort of noise. "You forget yourself."

I blinked as if slapped.

Now, it is true that back east it was considered very poor manners for young ladies, or any ladies for that matter, to discuss politics with men. But I had learned that many of the habits that ladies kept back east were of little use here on the frontier.

There was a long moment of silence at the table.

William wore a smug, superior look. Sally looked as if she rather wanted to burst into laughter, and the Hosmers seemed genuinely embarrassed by my behavior. But it was the expression on Mrs. Frink's face that gave me courage. Mrs. Frink was most certainly a lady who spoke her mind. She gave me a small, encouraging smile and I took a deep breath.

"Well, Mr. Biddle," I began in a civil tone. "We have lived quite agreeably with the Chinook for several years. Why, Mr. Swan is a longtime resident of Shoalwater Bay, and I'm quite sure he can, *as a gentleman*, second my opinion."

Mr. Swan looked momentarily flustered and then said in a loud voice, "Miss Peck is quite right. We enjoy a good relationship with the Chinook. In truth, we owe much of our prosperity to their continued friendship."

"All this talk of savages is making me rather faint," Mrs. Biddle said in a soft, protesting voice to her husband.

Mr. Biddle shot me a look, as if I were at fault for his wife's weak constitution. I wanted to tell him that she wouldn't faint if she ate something!

I stood up abruptly, clearing the plates for dessert.

Back in the kitchen, Millie said, "That was some conversation you were having over there."

"You give your opinions very freely," I mimicked as I angrily sliced the molasses pies onto plates.

Millie's eyes sparkled. "Maybe your pie will sweeten their tempers." She started to pile the plates on her tray. "I'll take care of the rest of the room if you get the head table."

I doubted very much that anything as simple as a

pie would sweeten Mrs. Biddle's temperament, or that of her husband. But Millie was correct about my pies. The dark, rich inside did look delicious.

I sliced the last remaining two pies, added a generous spoonful of fresh cream to each plate, and returned with my tray to the dining room.

Mrs. Frink stood up and announced to the room, "You are all in for a treat. Jane has baked us her famous pies!"

The room burst into applause and the men hooted.

"Why else do ya think we come here?" one man shouted back playfully.

I blushed and sat down.

"Your pie looks lovely, as usual, my dear," Mr. Swan said, and then took a hearty bite.

Around the room the guests were digging into their slices, and I tucked into my own piece. But no sooner had the pie hit my tongue than I knew something was wrong. Terribly wrong.

Mrs. Frink's eyes met mine helplessly, and she brought her napkin up to her mouth.

Mr. Swan was valiantly trying to swallow his bite, and William had started to cough. Sally looked absolutely pained, and Mr. Biddle hastily drained his glass of water.

But it was Mrs. Biddle, ever the lady, who unceremoniously spat out her mouthful onto her handkerchief. "It tastes like—like—," she sputtered, her lips pasted with crumbs.

I spit out my own mouthful and studied the rich, brown filling. Was that a piece of a worm?

"Like—like—"

"Mud," I finished.

"Mud!" Mrs. Biddle shrieked.

And then toppled to the floor in a dead faint.

CHAPTER SEVEN

or,

Stolen Goods

We discovered the culprit the next morning.

Willard was curled up in a tangle of sheets, moaning in agony from a terrible stomachache. He had eaten the rich molasses filling out of two of the pies and then cleverly replaced the molasses with mud, thinking no one would be the wiser. Brandywine had apparently participated in the crime and lay nestled next to Willard in the linen closet, where they had spent the night hiding. Millie had discovered them when she went to fetch fresh sheets.

"Will you look at the thieving bandits," Millie declared.

"Willard Woodley!" I said sternly.

"I'm sorry, Miss Jane," Willard said, clutching his stomach.

Brandywine whimpered piteously.

"Willard, you are more trouble than you are worth!"

He shook his head mournfully and blinked up at me, his face pale. He looked very much as if he were about to be sick all over the clean linen. "My belly hurts bad, Miss Jane!"

"Well, of course it does! You ate two pies' worth of molasses!" I said.

"You're lucky you haven't been sick all night," Millie added.

"But I have," he admitted glumly, pointing to a bundle of soiled sheets in the corner.

"Oh, for heaven's sakes. As if we don't have enough work around here already." I extended a hand. "Come on now, let's get you cleaned up, and then I'm taking you home to your mother."

Millie and I gave the boy a bath, which he was very unhappy about, and also some weak tea to settle his stomach. When he was feeling a little better, I took him by the hand and led him from the hotel.

As we made our way along Front Street, I noticed sly glances from several men we passed and heard soft snickering. As usual a group of men was loitering on the whiskey barrels in front of the bowling alley. They started guffawing in earnest when they saw me coming.

"Well, lookee. It's Jane Peck! Got any of that pie lying around, Jane?" one of them cackled.

I blushed so hard, I swear my cheeks were redder than my hair!

"Heard you made a real good pie last night, Miss Peck," another one laughed.

"Here's mud in your eye!" Red Charley shouted, taking a swig of whiskey.

"Willard," I scolded, utterly humiliated. "Look what you did!"

"The pie *was* good," Willard said in a mutinous voice.

I glared at him, and he managed to look sheepish.

"I ain't never gonna do that again, Miss Jane," Willard promised in a solemn voice.

"That is most certainly true, because you are fired," I informed him.

Willard looked stricken. "You can't fire me, Miss Jane! I don't wanna go back to working for that Mrs. Dodd. She's real mean, and I hate doing laundry. Honest, I'm real sorry," he whispered, hanging his head like Brandywine did sometimes. "You're not gonna tell my ma, are ya? She'll whip me for sure."

"Of course I'm going to tell your mother. She's probably been worried sick about you," I said firmly.

The door to Willard's house opened on the first knock.

"Oh, Miss Peck!" Mrs. Woodley exclaimed in surprise, and then her eyes shifted to her green-looking son. "Where have you been, Willard? Your pa was out looking for you half the night. You're gonna be feeling the end of his belt when he gets home."

One of his four little sisters squirmed through the open door and said in a smug voice, "You're gonna get a whipping, Willard!"

Willard looked up at me beseechingly, and I relented.

"Willard was helping me with a large supper party, and it finished quite late, so I suggested he sleep at the hotel. I assumed it would be fine, but I should have, of course, asked your permission."

Mrs. Woodley's round face softened. "Oh, well, that's a different story then. We were just so worried, with the thief and all."

"Thief?"

She gave me a puzzled look. "Surely you've heard, Miss Peck. The whole town's talking about it."

"About what?" I asked.

"Star's Dry Goods, of course."

"It got robbed!" another of the Woodley girls said as she shoved forward.

"By a thief!" yet another little girl piped up.

"Someone stole a cask of whiskey during the night," Mrs. Woodley explained, trying to corral her brood back into the cabin. "Can you believe it? A whole cask of whiskey!" She gave a wry smile. "At least we know it's a man."

"Did anyone see anything?" I asked.

Willard's mother was shaking her head vigorously.

"Apparently Mr. and Mrs. Staroselsky slept right through it. Can you imagine the boldness of a man to steal an entire barrel from right under their roof!"

Actually, I could, I thought, considering a certain hairy fellow.

"I see," I said with a forced smile. "Will you excuse me please? I need to get back to the hotel."

"See you at the sewing circle!" she called.

I moved as quickly as I could down the walkway, dodging men and comments about my pie-making abilities. By the time I reached the hotel, my heart was pounding.

Mrs. Frink was sitting in the parlor, studying a ledger.

"Jane?" she called in concern. "Is everything all right?"

But I had to see, right then. I ran straight past her, down the long hallway, and flung open the door to the storage room.

Hairy Bill's pallet was empty, and his things were missing.

He was gone!

News of what quickly became known as The Most Hideous Crime on Shoalwater Bay swept through town, and by suppertime it was all anyone was talking about. Stealing, all decided, was bad enough. Stealing whiskey, the men unanimously agreed, was an unforgivable offense.

"Jane," Mrs. Frink murmured to me. "I see that our furry guest is missing."

"Yes," I said. "He left yesterday. He told me to thank you very much for your kind hospitality."

She studied me. "You don't think he had anything to do with the theft at Star's?"

My face crumpled a little. "I certainly hope he didn't."

Over the following days speculation as to the identity of the thief ran rampant. Red Charley said that it was all a plot by the British to scare the Americans off the bay. Mr. Staroselsky insisted that he had heard the voices of two men talking, not one. William contended that the whiskey had no doubt been taken by Indians and if it happened again he was sending a letter to the governor. Everywhere I went, I feared I would find a drunk Hairy Bill curled up in a corner, but it seemed that he had well and truly cleared out, like a ghost in the night.

Whiskey and Hairy Bill, however, were not the only things that were missing.

Mrs. Biddle appeared before me in the parlor one morning, with Sally hovering behind her.

"I am most distressed," she announced in a quivery voice.

I looked up from my desk. "What can I help you with, Mrs. Biddle?"

She took a deep, shuddering breath. "I have been robbed!"

My stomach fell.

"Robbed?" I said. Mrs. Biddle and Sally had a great quantity of jewelry, I knew, and I couldn't help but picture Hairy Bill covered in pearls and rubies.

"Yes, robbed!" Mrs. Biddle insisted, wagging her head frantically.

Sally seemed to relish my discomfort.

"May I inquire as to what has been taken?" I asked.

Mrs. Biddle thrust a single glove at me. "There! There's the proof. I feel weak," she said, and collapsed into a chair, hand on her waist.

I studied the glove for a moment. It was a very nice glove. Finally I looked up.

"I'm sorry," I said. "But I don't understand. What does this glove have to do with being robbed?"

Mrs. Biddle fixed her eyes on me and said waspishly, "I should've thought it would have been perfectly obvious. Its match was stolen!"

"The glove was stolen?" I echoed.

"Yes! Are you deaf? There were two, and now there is only one. I left them with my other clothes to be laundered, and now one of the gloves is missing! Those are very expensive gloves!"

"And I am missing a stocking," Sally added.

"A stocking," I murmured. "I see."

"Well?" Mrs. Biddle demanded in a haughty voice.

"What are you going to do about this? I can't possibly wear one glove."

"Or one stocking," Sally said.

"Perhaps it is still at the laundress's," I suggested in a reasonable voice. "I'll look into it immediately."

"I should hope so." Mrs. Biddle huffed and turned. "Come along, Sally dear."

As the two ladies walked away, I heard Mrs. Biddle say, "Really, it is so hard to find decent help!"

Mrs. Dodd, the laundress for the hotel, was the wife of a stony-faced, hardworking oysterman. They were an older couple, with no children, and were originally from Maine. Mrs. Dodd in particular was very temperamental, but then doing laundry could do that to a person.

When I reached Mrs. Dodd's at the other end of town, I heard shouting before I even opened the door to the cramped-looking little cabin. The strong scent of lye hung in the air.

"You can't quit and leave me with all this work!" Mrs. Dodd shouted. "You work for me, you got that? I make the rules!"

"*Wēk!*" a voice said firmly. *Wēk* meant *no*.

The door opened abruptly and a young Chinook woman walked past me, her face set.

Mrs. Dodd shouted after her. "And I ain't paying you for this week, you hear me?"

"Good afternoon, Mrs. Dodd," I said uncertainly.

Mrs. Dodd was a stout woman with thin graying hair pulled back from her forehead in a damp mess. Her apron was streaked with thick brown stains, and I half shuddered, imagining what they might be. But it was her hands that gave me pause. They were a bright red from the lye soap and hot water required for washing.

"Second one I lost this month." She wagged her finger after the departing young woman. "Them savages won't work hard, that's their problem. They're lazy!" She turned on me with a snarl. "What da ya want? If you're looking for Willard, he ain't here. He's probably running after that half-breed girl."

I almost said, "What half-breed girl?" when I realized that she must have been referring to Katy, M'Carty and Cocumb's daughter. It made me wince to hear Katy described in such a manner, no matter how often I might hear people like Mrs. Dodd and Mrs. Biddle speak unkindly—and unfairly—about the Chinook.

I forced a smile. "Actually, I'm not looking for Willard. I just wanted to speak with you for a moment about the laundry for the hotel."

"Come on in," she said, opening her door reluctantly. "I don't have all day. I have twice the work now, thanks to her."

The cabin was a ramshackle mess. Filthy laundry lay heaped in piles, and the smell of the unwashed clothing combined with the harsh scent of lye was so powerful that I had to hold my breath for a moment. Clotheslines hung haphazardly back and forth across the cabin. It was nearly impossible on Shoalwater Bay to hang clothes out to dry, what with the eternal rain, and so the Dodds were obliged to live with other people's laundry hanging from the rafters of their small cabin. It was little wonder that Mrs. Dodd was temperamental.

I followed her, ducking under a wet sock.

"One of our guests has had some clothing go missing from her laundry. A white glove," I called after her. "Oh, and a stocking."

"Are you 'cusing me of being a thief?" she barked.

"Of course not," I said, waving a hand at the mess of clothes. "Perhaps it's hanging somewhere in here? Maybe it's still drying?"

Her face was set like a belligerent bulldog's. "You know how much laundry I do? I wash the clothes for that whole hotel and all these men, and I ain't got no help! And I tell you right here and now I ain't being paid nearly enough for all my troubles. Why, my man says I should be charging double for all the work I'm doing for the hotel. My man says—"

I blanched. Charge double? This was not going well at all.

"I understand completely," I said soothingly. "It's just that this is a rather important guest, and I thought I'd—"

"You thought you'd come over here with your hoity-toity ways and accuse me of stealing, didn't ya?"

"Not at all," I said nervously. "I just thought it might have been misplaced in all the"— I almost said "mess" but caught myself in time—"work."

She waved a red, bony finger in my face. "If you don't like how I do the laundry, you can take it somewhere else!"

As I stood there pressed against a damp sheet that smelled of old dog, I reconsidered my earlier opinion of Mrs. Dodd. Mrs. Dodd wasn't temperamental.

She was terrifying!

"You're perfectly right. So sorry to take up your valuable time," I said quickly, stumbling backward through the door.

"I've a good mind to let you do the laundry yourself!" Mrs. Dodd shouted, following after me.

I smiled overly widely. "Oh no, please, we're just thrilled with your work."

"Humph," she said. Then she turned and stomped away.

As I watched Mrs. Dodd waddle back inside, I complimented myself on discovering the location of Mrs. Biddle's missing white glove.

It was stuck to the sole of Mrs. Dodd's muddy shoe.

or,

A Barrel of Trouble

A break in the case of the whiskey thief came the next morning.

Willard came running into the kitchen, breathing hard. "There's been another robbery! But they caught the thief this time! He was trying to steal whiskey from Mr. Russell, and Mr. Russell caught him red-handed! There's gonna be a trial at Star's!"

Mrs. Frink and I stared at each other.

"What does he look like?" I asked.

He scratched his head. "I dunno. Like a normal fella, I reckon."

"Is he . . ." I swallowed. "Hairy?"

Willard scrunched up his face at me. "Hairy? Whadya mean? Like he don't shave?"

"You ought to go take a look, Jane," Mrs. Frink suggested.

"Come along, Willard," I said, and we started down the street.

"He's been locked in Mr. Russell's cowshed," Willard said. "They're gonna hang 'im!"

"Willard," I said in exasperation. "They're not going to hang a man over a barrel of whiskey."

He nodded his head vigorously. "They sure will, Miss Jane. All the men been saying that stealing whiskey's a hanging offense if ever there was one!"

By the time we reached Star's, a large crowd had already gathered and was spilling out the door. Clearly no oysters would be harvested this day, for it seemed that every unwashed oysterman in the territory had decided to observe the spectacle. Star's often stood in for a public meeting place, as we had no proper courthouse. Two men carrying a large barrel preceded me up the steps and into the store.

"This way," Willard whispered, and I held on to the boy's shirt as he pushed his way through the throng, deliberately stepping on men's feet. Amazingly, the crowd parted in the wake of Willard's single-minded attack, and he pulled me over to the wooden counter and nimbly hopped up.

"Come on," he urged. "You can see everything up here!"

I climbed up gingerly onto the counter and took a seat. He was right. The counter gave a perfect view of the proceedings. There were Mrs. Woodley and her husband and their girls, who were hopping up and down trying to see what was going on. Mrs. Hosmer gave me a little wave from the other side of the room, where she stood next to her adoring husband. Red Charley and his cohorts stumbled in, looking drunk as usual. He blew me an elaborate kiss.

Mr. Staroselsky was behind the counter doing a brisk business selling coffee and biscuits to the waiting crowd as Mrs. Staroselsky tried to calm a fractious Rose. Farther up front, Mr. Russell sat on a bench, chewing tobacco, and next to him was M'Carty, who had an arm around Cocumb. Behind them sat Father Joseph and Auntie Lilly. Even Mrs. Dodd was there, with her equally dour husband next to her. At the rear of the store, William entered with Mr. Biddle at his side. Right on their heels came Jehu and Keer-ukso.

Jehu met my eyes across the room. I saw a hint of wariness in his gaze and wondered at the cause. I rather abruptly remembered what had happened the last time I had seen him, and smiled to assure him all was well. His blue eyes immediately filled with warmth.

Suddenly a man shouted, "They're bringing him in!"

I closed my eyes. I could not bear to see Hairy Bill in chains.

"Look, Miss Peck. Thar's the fella. He ain't too hairy," Willard said.

My eyes snapped open and I found myself staring not at Hairy Bill, but at another man I vaguely recognized. The man in question was well trussed with rope and had great dark circles under his eyes. He had a gold tooth and a bald head.

It came to me at once that this was the man who had been lingering behind the hotel with his friend that evening. By the barrels, no less. No doubt they had been intending to steal them, too. I felt a pang of real regret for thinking Hairy Bill the thief.

Two burly men hauled the culprit through the parting crowd to the front of the room, where Mr. Swan was already sitting at a makeshift desk. They pushed the fellow down onto an upturned wooden box and stood on either side of him to prevent his escape.

"Order, order!" Mr. Swan called, banging his pipe on the desk.

Mr. Swan waited until the room was quiet and cleared his throat. "Now, we have gathered here concerning the matter of a cask of stolen whiskey, a particularly grave offense, as I'm sure you'll all agree."

"Hang 'im!" Red Charley shouted from the back.

"Whip 'im!" another cried.

I rather doubted there would even have been a trial if the fellow had stolen a cask of molasses.

"Yes, well, before we settle on the punishment, we must first bring charges against this gentleman, called . . . ," and at this Mr. Swan squinted at the paper before him. "Bowman? Is that your name, man?"

"It is, and what of it?" the man said belligerently.

"Have you a Christian name?"

"I already told you my name is Bowman."

Mr. Swan pushed his spectacles up on his nose. "Very well. Perhaps, Mr. Russell, if you could be so kind as to relate the events that transpired last evening?"

Mr. Russell stood up and glared at the man with the gold tooth. "This here feller stole my whiskey. Caught him rolling it away last night."

"And that would be the barrel I see before me?" Mr. Swan queried.

"Yep, that thar's the barrel," Mr. Russell said, and spit a wad of tobacco. "It's got my mark on the bottom."

The crowd rumbled angrily.

"Very good. And what happened when you caught him?" Mr. Swan prompted.

"Well, I had my rifle on me, so I jest stuck it in his back and locked him in my cowshed. Ain't no jail on the bay anyhow."

That was true enough. The usual punishment for offenders was banishment, which generally worked. Except when they returned, as in Hairy Bill's case.

"It ain't right, I tell you!" the man called Bowman howled. "Putting a fella in with a cow. Ain't civilized at all."

"Seems to me Burton got the bad end of the stick. Can't rightly see how she got a lick of sleep all night with you hollerin'," Mr. Russell said.

It did sound rather inhumane. Burton the cow was a snappish beast who had once bitten off a chunk of my hair when I tried to milk her. I couldn't imagine having to spend the night in the shed with that animal.

"I wasn't stealing nothing. You can't prove it!" Bowman shouted.

"I can prove a lot with this," Mr. Russell growled, brandishing his rifle.

"I tell ya I didn't steal that thar whiskey!" Bowman said in righteous indignation. "Fact is, I *caught* the feller who was stealing it. Why, I was jest bringing it back to ya!"

"My good man, you shall have an opportunity to speak in due time," Mr. Swan said.

Mr. Russell snorted at Bowman's flimsy defense. "Then why were ya going in the opposite direction?"

The man reddened, and then his eyes narrowed. "I'm new here and don't know my way around. And 'sides, it was dark, and I couldn't see hide nor hair of anything."

"Ya saw my whiskey jest fine," Mr. Russell said scornfully.

"I tell ya I was bringin' it back, not stealin' it!" Bowman shouted.

"Yar a thief, and a liar," Mr. Russell said, and there were assenting murmurs from the crowd.

"They're gonna hang 'im!" Willard whispered to me.

A sly gleam entered the doomed man's eye. "An Injun was stealing it! Why, I'd jest scared him off when you came along."

The crowd went hush-quiet at this pronouncement.

"Really, sir," Mr. Swan began uncomfortably.

Bowman turned in his chair, craning his neck, looking desperately into the crowd, eyes scanning the room. "Why, it was that Injun right there!"

I gasped.

The man was pointing at Keer-ukso!

"That is preposterous," Mr. Swan sputtered.

"It was that Injun there. The tall one!" the man shouted, his bald head bobbing enthusiastically.

And in that moment it was as if the entire room turned at once to stare at Keer-ukso. I saw murmured suspicion roll through the crowd, like an unstoppable wave, from man to man.

"Do you have any witnesses?" Mr. Swan asked.

"You bet I do! I got two good eyes, and they both saw that there Injun steal the whiskey!" Bowman shouted.

"You are lying," Keer-ukso spit.

Jehu stared at the accused man. "Keer-ukso was helping me fix my roof last night. He wasn't anywhere near Russell's cabin."

"You know how crazy those Injuns are for whiskey!" Bowman insisted.

There was a long, hushed silence in the room, and Keer-ukso stood perfectly still as eyes roamed over him.

"I believe Mr. Bowman has a point," William said. "And what kind of community is this that we take the word of a savage over that of an honest settler?"

I saw Keer-ukso flinch at these words. It was more than I could take.

"An honest settler?" I cried. "We don't even know who he is! Furthermore, that man was behind the hotel the other evening trying to steal *our* whiskey. And he would have taken it, too, if I hadn't caught him!"

"You tell him, gal!" Red Charley shouted.

"Miss Peck," William said, "I don't believe this is a matter of concern for young ladies."

I was shocked to be upbraided by William so publicly. And he wasn't the only one who thought my outspokenness was inappropriate. I received a dark look from Mr. Biddle as well.

"Furthermore," William declared, "I assure you that these raids by local Indians will continue unless we do something about them immediately. There have been reports of Indian uprisings throughout the territory. In fact, I believe we should begin building a fort to protect ourselves from future attacks, and arm all men—"

"Now that's enough!" M'Carty shouted, banging his rifle on the floor. He leaped to his feet and whirled on the crowd.

"On what authority do you speak, sir?" William demanded.

"On the authority of me being here before you, that's what authority," M'Carty said, glaring at William, and in an instant the crowd shifted.

William stood his ground. "I am the governor's man, and—"

"I know who you are, Baldt, and I don't care one bit," M'Carty interrupted him. "We don't cotton to interlopers coming and telling us what to do, you hear me? We make our own law round here."

Hoots and cheers broke out at this, and William's expression tightened.

M'Carty looked out at the crowd. "Besides Russell, I've been here the longest, and you all know how I feel about these things. Now if Russell, Jehu, and Jane all say that this here feller stole the whiskey, then it seems good sense that we take their word for it."

"But that Injun stole the whiskey!" Bowman protested.

"Feller, I don't know what rock you crawled out from under, but I do know one thing, and it's that you've got a real slimy tongue," M'Carty said. "Now you better believe me when I tell you Russell and I have scared off our share of grizzly bears and you don't hold a candle to them."

"Least the bears smell better," said Mr. Russell with a chuckle.

There was nervous laughter from the crowd.

M'Carty looked around the store. "All you folks know that we haven't had any trouble with the Indians. Fact is, most of you wouldn't have two coins to rub together if they hadn't helped you with your oyster beds."

"He's got a squaw as a wife," Bowman said desperately. "Can't trust a man who lies down with savages!"

M'Carty had his rifle up and under the fellow's chin so fast that no one breathed.

"Let me tell you something, feller. In case you don't got eyes, that beautiful woman is my wife, and that gentleman you accused is my family, and when you go after them, you're going after me. So you better think twice before you start spouting wild accusations, because I'm not about to let a lying, no-account fellow like you go around hurting my people. You got that? And they are *my people*," M'Carty said in a dangerously low voice.

Little beads of sweat broke out on Bowman's forehead.

"I've said my piece," M'Carty said after a long moment, and sat down, wrapping a comforting arm around Cocumb.

But some indefinable thing had happened, and while I could see that most in the room took M'Carty's word, I also saw skepticism on a few faces.

"Thank you, M'Carty," Mr. Swan said. "I'm afraid, sir, that if you have no other witnesses to present, then I shall have to make my ruling." He stared at Bowman, but the man just shook his head. "Very well. It is clear to me based on the testimony of Mr. Russell, Mr. Scudder, and Miss Peck that the accused is guilty of the charges against him."

Bowman muttered, "It ain't right."

"Now," Mr. Swan began. "I am inclined to be lenient as this is a first offense. And also because no harm came to the whiskey. It would be another matter entirely if the whiskey had been drunk." He grinned.

The men in the room chuckled.

Mr. Swan regarded the accused. "Mr. Bowman, you are hereby sentenced to spend one night in jail. But as we have no jail, and you did spend one night in Mr. Russell's cowshed, it shall be considered time served. Therefore, I am ordering you to depart Shoalwater Bay and never darken its shores again."

"There's a schooner leaving for San Francisco this afternoon," Jehu said helpfully.

M'Carty and Mr. Russell walked up to Bowman and stood over him.

"Whadya say we put him on the boat ourselves, Obediah?" M'Carty asked with a scornful look at the thief.

Mr. Russell spit. "Reckon that's a real fine idea. Wouldn't want him to get lost, now would we?"

Bowman glared at them.

Mr. Swan banged down hard on the desk.

"Court adjourned!"

CHAPTER NINE

The Contest

The sewing circle was meeting the next afternoon, and with Sally Biddle attending, I wanted to look my best. I had several dresses to choose from, and while they were not nearly as grand as anything in Sally's trunks, I was rather proud of having sewn them all myself—no easy feat.

In the end I chose a pale blue calico frock, with an edge of lace at the collar and about the wrists that I had scavenged from an old napkin. As I dressed for tea, I recalled the day I had won the embroidery contest at the Young Ladies Academy. Miss Hepplewhite had declared that I had the neatest small stitch of any pupil who'd ever attended the academy. Sally had been stunned at my victory. Even now my heart swelled with pride at the remembered triumph. It was the only time

I had ever bested Sally at anything.

On my way out the door, I was stopped by Mrs. Frink.

"Oh Jane, I won't be able to attend the tea this afternoon. Will you please give my regrets to Mrs. Staroselsky?"

"Are you not feeling well?" I asked, noticing her pale cheeks.

I worried about her sometimes. She had lost her only child on the harsh trip overland, and while she never spoke of it, there were moments when her competent facade slipped and sadness crept across her features like a spreading stain.

She gave me a weary smile. "Just a bit tired."

A misty rain had begun to fall, and in my haste I had neglected to bring one of my newest coveted treasures for the walk to Mrs. Staroselsky's—my parasol. I had no doubt my hair would be a fuzzy, frizzy mess by the time I reached the tea.

As I strolled along the walkway, I looked out at the bay. Workers were loading a schooner with a fresh haul of oysters for shipment to San Francisco. There would be gold in many men's pockets this evening, and most of it would be in Red Charley's by tomorrow.

I went around Star's to the little cabin where the Staroselskys lived and knocked on the door. My heart lightened at the familiar sound of feminine laughter drifting out the windows.

"Hello, Jane," Mrs. Staroselsky said, her mouth widening in a smile. She was bobbing a blanket-wrapped bundle in her arm that let out a squawk every few moments. "We'd almost given up hope that you were coming!"

"I'm so sorry I'm late," I began as I peered around her at the ladies gathered beyond the door.

Sally, outfitted in a walking dress of rose silk with a flounced skirt and a charming matching bonnet bearing a profusion of silk roses, was holding court in the middle of the Staroselskys' cabin, a cup of tea in hand, as if she were in the finest parlor in Philadelphia!

"The sailors spent all their time flirting shamelessly with us ladies," Sally was telling her attentive audience. "Naturally, we ignored their advances. But the most incredible thing was that a number of these men already had wives!"

"No!" Mrs. Hosmer gasped.

"In every port," Sally added drolly.

"Watch out, Jane," Mrs. Woodley teased, explaining to Sally, "She's courting a sailor."

"A captain," I clarified.

"I thought you said he was first mate," Mrs. Staroselsky said.

"He was first mate on my voyage here, but then he was hired as captain."

"Is this the gentleman who brought our luggage to the hotel?" Sally asked.

I nodded.

"And you met him on a ship?" Sally asked in a considering voice.

"Yes," I said, and flushed despite myself.

"A word of advice then, as one lady to another," Sally said, her voice full of sisterly warmth, kindness itself. "You should be careful with your affections regarding this man. He may already be married."

"Jehu would never do anything like that," I said.

"Of course, you know him best," Sally agreed, her voice dripping with sympathy. She turned a winning smile on the hostess. "May I have some more cake, Mrs. Staroselsky? It is simply delicious."

"Anything without oysters is delicious, if you ask me," Mrs. Hosmer confided. "I have eaten more oysters in my short time here on the bay than all the rest of my life!"

All of a sudden, Rose's mewling cries echoed through the modest cabin.

"Come now, you must be tired, sweetheart," Mrs. Staroselsky said, rocking the baby back and forth in her arms in a determined way. She turned to the group in exasperation. "All she does is cry. Do you have any suggestions, Jane?" She held the small, screaming bundle out to me.

Papa's clientele had tended toward drunken sailors who cracked open their heads during bar brawls, not babies.

"I don't have much experience with babies," I said.

"Poor mite," Mrs. Woodley said with a sympathetic cluck. "Probably teething. Try rubbing whiskey on her gums."

"Whiskey?" Mrs. Staroselsky asked.

Mrs. Woodley shrugged with all the experience of a lady who had held many a fussing baby. "Only thing whiskey's good for, in my opinion."

The ladies chuckled.

"Here, let me," Mrs. Woodley said, taking the baby with sure hands. "Fetch me a teacup with a tablespoon of whiskey."

We all watched as Mrs. Woodley rubbed a little whiskey on the baby's gums, and after a moment the child's sobs softened to a tired hiccup.

"There, there," Mrs. Woodley said, and walked the baby across the room to the small cradle. Mrs. Hosmer and Mrs. Staroselsky trailed behind her to admire the now calm baby, leaving Sally and me alone at the table.

"Would you care for a cup of tea, Jane?" Sally asked, extending a freshly poured cup.

I hesitated for a moment, recalling the last time I had accepted a beverage from her. Finally I took the tea from her with unsteady hands.

"Careful, Jane," Sally murmured in a low voice. "You wouldn't want tea stains on your new frock. It is a new frock, isn't it? And my, what an unusual style. I believe I saw our maid wearing something like it. Is that a napkin sewn to the cuff? How clever."

The ladies walked back over to us.

"Now what were you two discussing?" Mrs. Hosmer asked eagerly.

"Fashion," Sally said.

"You'll have to have Jane make you a dress!" Mrs. Woodley said. "Our Jane's a marvel with a needle and thread. Why, she sewed the dress I'm wearing! Mr. Woodley thinks it's one of the nicest gowns I've ever owned. He says it complements my figure."

I shot Sally a triumphant look. The tables had turned. She was on *my* territory now!

"Do you remember when I won the embroidery contest at Miss Hepplewhite's?" I asked.

Sally returned my challenging stare. "How could I forget?"

Mrs. Staroselsky, who seemed vastly relieved by the fact that her baby was finally dozing off, asked, "Where is Mrs. Frink, Jane?"

"I'm afraid she wasn't feeling well. Which reminds me, I was thinking it might be nice to invite Cocumb to join us next time."

"Cocumb? What an unusual name. Is she French?" Sally asked.

"No," I said. "She's Chinook."

Sally's eyes widened in surprise. "She's an Indian?"

"And she's a very dear friend of mine," I said. I was not about to let Sally Biddle of all people besmirch Cocumb's character.

There was a moment's silence, and then Sally uttered in a sympathetic voice, "Why, that's terribly brave of you, Jane."

"Brave? There's nothing to be brave about," I said a little too loudly. My voice seemed to bounce off the walls of the cabin.

The other ladies looked between us.

Sally took a careful sip of tea and said in an offhand way, "It's just all the news back east."

"What news?" Mrs. Hosmer asked.

"About the sickness, of course," Sally began delicately. "The news sheets are full of the accounts. Pioneers on the trail catching cholera and other horrible diseases from Indians. Whole families have died. It's tragic. Children are apparently the most susceptible."

Mrs. Staroselsky's gaze flicked over to the quiet cradle, and the cabin seemed to hum with fear.

"Physicians are recommending limiting contact if possible." Sally paused deliberately, turning to me. "I seem to recall hearing your father mentioning something similar."

I stared at her. That had been Papa's opinion. He never let me near patients who had cholera or smallpox.

"Jane," Mrs. Hosmer began in a nervous voice, "wasn't there an epidemic last year? Isn't that how your little friend Sootie lost her mother?"

All eyes were on me, and my tongue seemed to swell in my mouth.

"But it wasn't their fault, and this is the frontier. If we'd had proper medical . . ." I let my voice trail off.

There was an uncomfortable moment of silence as all the women looked down at their laps.

All except Sally, who smiled at me and said, "That's precisely what I'm saying. You're so *very* brave, Jane."

I remained behind a few moments to help Mrs. Staroselsky tidy up, and by the time I left for the hotel, the rain was simply pounding down. I had no sooner placed my foot onto the walkway when my boots hit a slippery bit of wood and went out from under me, and I found myself tumbling into the muddy road. I sat there for a moment, too stunned to move.

"You all right there, Miss Peck?" Red Charley shouted from across the street.

I most certainly was not all right! I looked as if I had bathed in mud!

Gathering as much dignity as I could muster under the circumstances, I hefted my heavy, sodden, muddy skirts and made my way down the walkway to the hotel. As I drew nearer, I saw a broad, dark-haired man carrying a lady across a broken bit of plank.

The man looked suspiciously like Jehu.

I squinted hard through the pounding rain. It *was* Jehu!

And the lady he was so gallantly carrying was . . . Sally Biddle!

"Why hello, Jane!" Sally said, linking her arm comfortably around Jehu's tanned neck. Her eyes took in my muddy dress. "Oh dear, did you take a fall?"

Jehu shifted his weight and set her on the ground. Was it my imagination, or did his strong hands linger on her shoulders for a second?

"Isn't he the perfect gentleman?" Sally tittered, patting her hair with exaggerated care. "There I was on the other side of the street, and there was nothing but mud before me! I couldn't risk muddying this skirt. And this kind man came to my rescue! I can't thank you enough, Mr. Scudder," Sally finished, looking adoringly at Jehu.

Jehu swallowed and nodded.

"I do hope we have the opportunity to meet again," Sally said, holding out a dainty gloved hand.

Jehu looked at it in confusion for a moment and then shook it.

"Have a lovely day, Jane," Sally said smugly, and walked up the steps of the hotel.

or,

The Gathering Storm

Like an unwelcome guest, the rain came and stayed.

Fierce summer storms battered the bay. Front Street turned into a river, with the planks from the walkway floating by on the current. The tides grew so high that returning oystermen could sail right up to a tavern and have themselves a drink. Mrs. Woodley's home was set adrift one morning when her husband was out, and Mr. Frink and several other men went after it in boats. In order to rescue the cabin, they finally had to tie it to a piling. By this time, poor Mrs. Woodley and her girls were perched on a table, waist-deep in water and perfectly terrified.

The most popular topic at the supper table was the upcoming elections. Of the three races, the position of justice of the peace was the most hotly debated, with

Mr. Swan, William, and Red Charley all campaigning for that office. Red Charley had begun going around town handing out free whiskey to encourage votes. Mr. Frink was running for representative to the legislature, as was Mr. Dodd. M'Carty was the lone candidate running for constable, and everyone agreed he was a shoo-in because he was the best shot in the entire territory. Not to mention, no one else wanted the job.

Mrs. Biddle, who seemed personally offended by the wet weather, sat in the parlor complaining. She complained that the shouts of the men returning from drinking in the bowling alley kept her from falling asleep. The air did not agree with her and made her feel weak. The food we served at the hotel was not seasoned properly, and furthermore, the amenities in the rooms were not up to her usual standard. Her chief complaint, however, was the lack of amusements available in Shoalwater Bay.

"There is simply nothing to do here!" Mrs. Biddle declared, flouncing into the parlor in a rather unladylike way.

Finally, after many soggy days, the sun broke out, bathing the bay in glorious light. At the first chance, I fled Mrs. Biddle and the confines of the hotel and headed to the beach to breathe in the warm salty air blowing off the bay. Gulls swooped low, kissing the surface of the water. In the distance the oystermen readied their boats to head out. Farther down the beach Sootie and Katy were looking for treasures that might have washed up on shore from the storms.

Beachcombing was popular here, as many ships had the misfortune to wreck along this treacherous coast. They would become stranded along the bar and smash to bits in the ensuing storms. Sometimes we could see the doomed ships far out at sea, flickers of light in the pounding rain and darkness. The next morning the beach would be littered with wreckage and, sometimes, bodies.

Jehu, as the bay's pilot, had been designated wreckmaster by the locals. It was his responsibility to decide what to do with cargo washed up on the beach, which was how I had come by my gold silk dress. A bolt of gold silk had been packed in a camphor wood chest that had floated in with the tide. All manner of goods washed up on shore. Candles, casks of wine, sidesaddles, sacks of flour and raisins, and even a piano, which did not, admittedly, play very well after being adrift in the salty water. Several months earlier Mr. Swan had salvaged a cask of whiskey that had drifted to the shore unharmed. It was promptly drunk by the men.

"Boston Jane." Sootie waved her hand. "Look what we found."

I knelt down to inspect her treasure. It was a strange whitish lump.

"Do you know what it is?" Katy asked.

"It's beeswax," Jehu said.

I whirled around to see Jehu standing over us, blocking the sun, a grin on his tanned face.

"Beeswax?"

He squinted slightly, inspecting the object. "I've seen it on ships from the Orient before."

"Papa says the Orient is very far away," Katy said with authority. "He's sailed there."

Jehu knelt down and smiled at the little girl. "I've sailed to the Orient, too, and it is very far away." There was a soft note of longing in his voice.

"But how did it get here?" Sootie asked curiously.

"Could be a ship went down, somewhere out at sea. It probably floated out in the ocean for a long time. And then I reckon it heard about you lovely ladies, so it decided that this was a good place to come ashore," he teased them.

Katy and Sootie giggled.

"What do we do with it?" Katy asked.

"Maybe we can trade it with Mr. Staroselsky," Sootie said. "And get more fabric for dresses."

"Why don't we give it to Willard?" Katy suggested.

Sootie gave an indelicate snort. "Willard? Why would we give it to Willard?"

Jehu chuckled at this.

"Speaking of lovely ladies," Jehu said, straightening, "I've been looking for a certain redheaded one. I have something to show you."

He swung my hand in his and whistled as we walked down the beach in companionable silence. This, I thought, was true love. Someone who made you happy without saying a word.

We had reached the edge of his claim, and I saw that there were several stakes in the ground, as if marking off an area.

"This is where we're going to build the mill," Jehu said. "We can float logs down the bay, mill them here, and then load them on barges."

I surveyed the proposed site. "It's a very agreeable location."

He placed his hands on my shoulders and looked deep into my eyes. "Jane, I have some exciting news." He seemed about ready to burst.

"Go on," I encouraged him.

"I've been talking to Sally."

My heart skipped a beat.

"It's the answer to all our prayers."

"Sally Biddle is the answer to our prayers?" I asked hesitantly.

"Not Sally. Her father. Mr. Biddle."

"Jehu, I don't understand at all," I said, feeling a twinge of unease. What could Jehu want with Mr. Biddle?

"Sally said that her father's looking for good investments." He pointed at the land. "She thinks he might want to invest in the mill!"

"I see," I said, and I did. Mr. Biddle now was the wealthiest man on the bay. In truth, he was the only man on the bay who had capital to invest.

"Sally said she'd mention my idea to him," he continued. "And that she'd even arrange for me to meet with him!"

I'll just bet she did, I thought.

Jehu seemed genuinely puzzled by my lack of enthusiasm and gave me a little shake. "Don't you see, Jane? He might partner up with us. It's what we've been waiting for!"

Deep in the pit of my soul I knew that Mr. Biddle would never become partners with Jehu. Not Mr. Biddle with the fine house on Arch Street. Men of Mr. Biddle's class would never consider sailors as business partners.

"What do you think?" he asked eagerly.

I stared at the hope shining in his eyes.

"How wonderful, Jehu," I said with forced gaiety. "I'm so proud of you."

"Everything's gonna work out, Jane," he said fervently. "We'll be rich!"

He picked me up and whirled me around, kissing me soundly.

I couldn't help but remember Millie telling me that her husband had said the very same thing before he left for California.

❧

The kitchen was abuzz with preparations for supper when I returned to the hotel. Spaark was shucking oysters. When I walked in, her whole face lit up. She was wearing the same enthusiastic expression as Jehu had been.

"Boston Jane! Isn't it exciting?"

I just looked at her.

She pointed a finger up, indicating the guest rooms upstairs. "Keer-ukso, he told me about Mr. Biddle giving money."

"But Mr. Biddle might not give Jehu and Keer-ukso the money," I said. "They haven't even talked to him."

"He will give them the money," Spaark said.

I tried to smile but couldn't. This day that had begun so agreeably was getting worse by the moment. Finally I said, "I think I'll go and check on supplies."

Sitting at my little desk writing out a list did nothing to restore my sense of well-being. Was Sally orchestrating all this to get back at me? Did she plan to raise Jehu's hopes and then dash them cruelly? It seemed like something Sally would do.

A shadow fell over the desk and I glanced up. William stood there, looking every bit the refined gentleman.

"A moment of your time, Jane?" William said, wearing a thin smile.

"Trying to impress Mr. Biddle?" I asked, staring at his new suit.

Back in Philadelphia, William had always craved the finer things. But more than that, he had craved belonging to a better social class.

"I hardly need to try, Jane. I am not some lowly apprentice out here. Mr. Biddle recognizes me for the man of influence I am," he said with just a touch of impatience. He motioned to the parlor. "Shall we?"

I bit my lip and followed him to the parlor, where the late-afternoon light spilled in through the windows. He took a comfortable seat on the settee, perfectly at ease in my presence.

"Have you heard that I am running for justice of the peace?" he asked, his voice full of the old arrogance.

"So is Red Charley," I said dryly.

His lips twitched slightly, but then his face settled into the controlled mask I knew so well. How had I ever thought that this man sitting across from me deserved my affection?

"What do you want, William?" I asked.

"As you know, I am surveying land on behalf of . . . interested parties."

"What has that to do with me?" I said.

He shook his head as if I were a recalcitrant child. "Jane, Jane. You have acquired a rather sharp tongue. Something I don't approve of in the least."

"Your approval has not been my concern for some time," I said.

William pulled a slip of paper out of his jacket.

"This shall be of some concern to you, though, I should imagine."

Something in me went still at the sight of that paper. It looked so familiar.

"It is so interesting what one runs across when working for the governor," he said nonchalantly. "This came into my possession quite recently."

My eyes widened. It was my claim!

"GRANT FOR ONE HUNDRED AND TWENTY ACRES OF LAND TO J. PECK. DECEMBER 22, 1854."

He clucked his tongue sympathetically. "And I must say, I find it very curious indeed that an unmarried lady, barely older than a child, has a claim for some of the most timber-rich land on the bay, when government land grants are meant only for white men over the age of twenty-one," he said. "A rather fortuitous discovery, wouldn't you agree?"

My mind raced. Even now I remembered what Jehu had said after he'd filed the claim on my behalf, writing "J. Peck" because—

They'll never know. You could be a Jonathan or a Jack or a Jebediah—

"So under the law, one could legitimately assume that there are one hundred and twenty acres of unclaimed land around here, don't you think?" He leaned back, all confidence.

I stared at him in shocked silence. He had tricked me into coming out here, abandoned me, married another woman, and now he was threatening to take my land? I hadn't thought it was possible for him to sink any lower, but apparently it was!

Finally William said mockingly, "Why, Jane. I do believe this is the first time in all our acquaintance that you have nothing to say! How perfectly remarkable."

The door to the hotel opened, and I heard footsteps. Mr. Biddle was standing in the doorway.

"Shall we go see that piece of land you mentioned, William?" he asked. "The one you said was situated on a high bluff with good access to the bay?"

A high bluff with good access to the bay? That sounded suspiciously like *my* claim!

I looked at William, but he merely raised a mysterious eyebrow.

Mr. Biddle caught sight of me and said, "Good afternoon, Miss Peck."

"Mr. Biddle," I said.

William stood abruptly. "Miss Peck and I were just discussing a matter of mutual interest. I believe we have finished our conversation, haven't we, Miss Peck?" There was a challenging note in his voice.

I said nothing.

"Very good then," Mr. Biddle said with a touch of impatience. "Shall we be off?"

William shook his head at me in disappointment and said, "We shall finish this discussion later, Miss Peck."

As I watched the two of them stride down the hotel steps, I felt the firm ground being swept from beneath my feet, my whole safe world cast away. I was like one of those lost ships, tossed against jagged rocks, being sent to my doom.

CHAPTER ELEVEN

or,

Biddle's Gold

It soon became apparent that Jehu was not the only one with designs on Mr. Biddle's money.

All of a sudden every prospecting man on the bay began hanging about the hotel in hopes of talking Mr. Biddle into funding some wild scheme. Red Charley wanted Mr. Biddle to go in on opening a new tavern with him, Mr. Swan thought there were possibilities in salmon, and even Mrs. Frink was full of hopeful ideas.

"Mr. Frink and I have been speaking to Mr. Biddle about becoming a partner in the hotel," Mrs. Frink said, her voice laced with excitement. "With more funds, we could add a new wing and take in more guests."

Only Millie seemed to share my misgivings.

"It's like the gold rush," she said, shaking her head. "Men can't see what's right in front of them. They're too busy counting gold they haven't even dug up yet."

As for me, my thoughts were consumed with William's threats. When I tried to share my fears with Jehu, he dismissed them.

"Baldt's full of bluster," he said. "He just likes stirring you up. Ignore him."

But I knew that William wasn't full of bluster. He was full of greed.

I was waylaid by Father Joseph one afternoon as I walked toward M'Carty's homestead. I was finally getting around to returning the rifle Hairy Bill had brought back.

"Mademoiselle," he called as I strolled along Front Street.

"Father Joseph," I said, relief flooding me. Perhaps he could give me some good advice on how to deal with William. "I'm so happy to see you!"

"And I you," he said with a reassuring smile. "Where are you going?"

"To visit Cocumb and M'Carty," I explained.

"I'll go with you as far as the stream."

As we walked, a tired-looking oysterman passed us, his wagon piled perilously high with oysters. The wheel of the wagon hit a thick groove in the road and looked as if it was going to tip over, but then the man yelled at the horse and skillfully maneuvered it back to safety.

"Father, I need your advice about something," I said.

"But of course, and I've been meaning to ask your advice as well," he said with a tilt of his bald head.

"My advice?"

He met my eyes. "You are friends with Mademoiselle Biddle?"

"We are acquainted with each other," I said in a hesitant voice.

"Wonderful," he said. "I was hoping that you might arrange an introduction to her father."

"You want to talk to Mr. Biddle?"

"The chapel is in very poor repair," he explained. "And I am hoping that he might contribute some funds to build a new church."

My heart sank.

I promised Father Joseph I would try to arrange a meeting with Sally's father and bade him farewell, then continued through the woods to where M'Carty and Cocumb lived. It was a considerable walk from town, on the far edge of the bay.

Cocumb was sitting on the front porch of her cabin weaving a basket when I arrived at her homestead. "Hello, Boston Jane," she said with a smile.

Katy came running around from behind the house, carrying a handful of grass reeds. "Hello, Boston Jane," she said.

Cocumb smoothed her daughter's thick black hair, a mirror image of her own. "Katy and I are making a basket, aren't we, *nika tenas klootchman*?"

Nika tenas klootchman. My sweet little girl.

"It's very lovely," I said, surveying the basket. It had a figure of a crane woven into it.

"Come in. We have another visitor," Cocumb replied.

I saw the silhouette of a man sitting by the fire, and by the scraggly shape of his whiskers, I knew him immediately.

"Mr. Russell," I said, pleased.

"Gal," Mr. Russell said, spitting a huge wad of tobacco at my feet.

Mr. Russell was not a man given to good manners, I'm afraid, but he was M'Carty's oldest friend, and I imagined that Cocumb was rather used to him by now.

M'Carty was sitting right next to Mr. Russell in a beautifully carved rocking chair, smoking a pipe.

"Hello there, Miss Peck! What brings you way out here?"

"Hairy Bill was passing through and brought this back," I said, handing him the rifle.

"Huh. How about that." He restored the rifle to its place of honor on a hook over the fireplace.

"Please, sit down," Cocumb said.

I took a seat on one of the benches, and admired the cheery cabin. At one end was the fireplace, and near it a long, gleaming wood table. In another corner was the sleeping area, sectioned off with a length of canvas.

Cocumb perched on her husband's knee, and

M'Carty placed an affectionate hand on her waist.

"How's your oyster beds?" M'Carty asked.

"I'm afraid we haven't had time to harvest them," I admitted. "I was thinking I might rent them out for a season."

"Reckon I can find you someone who might be interested," he said. "I'm going to Astoria next week. Anything you want me to bring back?"

"Maybe you could take me with you?" I said, only half joking.

"Now why is that?" M'Carty asked.

"It's just that I wouldn't mind getting away from here for a little while," I confessed. Away from William and his threats, that is.

"What's the matter, gal?" Mr. Russell asked in a sharp voice, but I heard the concern underneath.

I explained the situation with William and my claim. M'Carty nodded as I spilled out my fears.

"Can he take my land?" I asked.

M'Carty's eyes met Mr. Russell's for a long moment.

"And to think I came here to get away from folks like Baldt," Mr. Russell grumbled.

"Jehu says I have nothing to worry about," I said. "Still, I can't help but think he's wrong."

M'Carty rocked slowly in his chair, puffing on his pipe. "Look, Jane, way I figure it, Baldt's gonna need some sort of legal writ or something to take that land away from you, and the only person who can give him that is a judge."

"That's what I'm afraid of! The elections. William's running for justice of the peace! What if he wins?"

"I reckon we should all be worrying about Red Charley winning," Mr. Russell scoffed. "There sure has been a lot of free whiskey going around lately."

"Do you think William has a chance of winning, Jane?" Cocumb asked, and by the look in her eye, I knew that she did not underestimate William. After all, he had tried to put her family on a reservation.

"I think he could win," I said. "He's got Mr. Biddle's ear. And everyone wants to get on Biddle's good side, so they might vote for him to get to Biddle. No one's going to vote for Red Charley, no matter how much whiskey he hands out for free."

M'Carty puffed on his pipe. "Is Biddle the fellow with all the money?"

"I met him," Mr. Russell growled. "He came sniffin' round the cabin with Baldt."

"Your cabin?" I asked.

"The man's speculating. Looking to grab up land. Offered me fifty dollars for my claim."

Fifty dollars was quite a lot of money, but even so, everyone who lived on the bay knew that Mr. Russell would rather die than sell his land.

"I don't trust Baldt," Cocumb said.

"And you got good instincts, *nayka klootchman*,"

M'Carty said, his eyes tender.

Nayka klootchman. My sweetheart.

I looked away, at the fire, embarrassed by their show of affection.

"So what do I do?" I asked.

There was a long moment as we contemplated the turn of events.

Finally Mr. Russell blurted out, "Bah! Don't you worry, gal. Me and M'Carty'll take care of things if it comes to that."

"You got that right, Russell. We got all the law we need right here." M'Carty looked at the rifle hanging over the fireplace and chuckled.

When I returned to the hotel it was quite late, and Jehu and Keer-ukso were sitting at the kitchen table with Mr. Frink, papers strewn before them, candles burning brightly.

"I think you'll need a few more men," Mr. Frink was saying as he reviewed what were obviously the plans for the mill.

"So we have to redo all the figures and start over again?" Jehu took a deep breath.

"Looks that way," Mr. Frink said.

"What's all this?" I asked.

"Sally suggested that I make up a real detailed plan for her father," Jehu said. "Lay out how many men we'll need, that sort of thing. Way I figure it, it's no different

133

than organizing a sailing crew, and I've done that plenty of times."

"Has Mr. Biddle agreed to meet with you?"

"Sally said that he was very busy right now, but she had no doubt that he would want to meet with us when the time is right," Jehu said, slapping his hat on his hand triumphantly. "That's practically a yes!"

"Jehu is very smart, Boston Jane," Keer-ukso said.

As I watched Jehu, a feeling of helplessness came over me. He wanted this so badly, yet I knew there was no way he was going to get Mr. Biddle's support. Sally was doing this to get at me. I recalled how our rivalry had started all those years ago.

I was eleven years old. On the fateful day, my friend, Jebediah Parker, and I had been challenged to an apple-throwing contest by two neighborhood boys, Horace Fink and Godfrey Hale. When my turn arrived, I chose a particularly rotten apple and threw it at the big tree on Arch Street.

At that exact moment Sally stepped out of her house.

My apple missed the tree completely and struck young Sally Biddle right on the bosom of her pale rose dress. From that moment forward, she tried everything in her power to make my life a misery.

Except we weren't children anymore, I suddenly realized. Nor were we in Philadelphia. Ladies were different out here. We were strong and hardworking, and we knew what counted. She had to be stopped.

I walked upstairs and knocked firmly on Sally's door.

"Come in," she called sweetly.

I must say, it felt very strange to be invited into my own room.

Sally was admiring herself in the mirror. "Jane! How lovely to see you."

"I know what you're doing, Sally," I said. "And I want you to leave Jehu alone."

Her eyes widened in an innocent expression. "What exactly am I doing?"

I snapped. "You know as well as I do that your father will never invest in Jehu's mill. Stop toying with him!"

She nodded thoughtfully. "Yes, well, I'm afraid that is true. Sailors aren't exactly the sort of gentlemen that Papa goes into business with."

"You are deliberately trying to hurt him! Why?" I demanded in exasperation.

Sally's face settled into a cold mask. "I should think it would be perfectly apparent why I am doing this." She paused deliberately. "Because of you."

"But this has gone on long enough! I never meant to throw that apple at you! It was a mistake!" I said wildly.

"What apple?"

"The apple that started it all. The one I threw at you when we were children."

"I have no idea what you're talking about."

I looked at her in bewilderment. "If it's not the apple, then why do you hate me so?"

Sally regarded my reflection in her mirror with distaste and fanned herself.

"You owe me an explanation!" I demanded.

She whirled on me, a look of pure malice on her face. "I don't owe you anything! You—you and your muddy aprons and uncombed hair. You were like a wild animal, always running around the streets with boys, playing your silly games."

Sally stalked over to me, waving her fan like a sword.

"And your doting father," she laughed contemptuously. "It was pathetic the way he talked about you all the time, acting as though he were proud of you throwing manure at carriages," she said, but I heard the jealousy in her voice. "After all that, you had the nerve to attend Miss Hepplewhite's as if you had a perfect right to be there." She curled her lips and growled. "I was her favorite student until you came."

I took a wary step back.

"Who do you think you are, anyway, Jane Peck?" she snarled.

"I—I—"

"When Father decided to come here, I had assumed that I would remain in Philadelphia. And then Father announced that I was to join him and Mother on the voyage," she spit out furiously. "I told him Cora Fletcher was quite happy to have me stay with her. But no. He would not hear of it. And do you know why?"

"Why?" I whispered.

"Sally dear, your friend Jane Peck will be there to keep you company!" she said, mimicking her father in a singsong voice.

"But—"

"I was supposed to be Horace Fink's wife!" Sally shouted. "He was planning to ask Father for my hand in marriage. But now, instead of being feted all over Philadelphia, I am stuck *here*," she said, her voice scathing. "Where there is nothing but rain and mud and oysters! If I never eat another oyster again it will be too soon."

"But it's not my fault!" I protested.

"Of course it's your fault. It's always been your fault. You've always been jealous of me. You've always conspired to bring me down to your level."

I stared at her in disbelief and confusion, and then she laughed merrily at me.

"Still, I admit it has been very enjoyable amusing myself with your sailor. For a man of the world, he is very gullible," she said.

She grinned at me as I stood there speechless.

"You have ruined my life," she said with a satisfied smile. "And I have every intention of ruining yours."

or,

The Power of Persuasion

I spent a restless night replaying Sally's words over and over again in my head. I kept hearing her say, *You have ruined my life. And I have every intention of ruining yours.*

But what could I do? Everyone else thought Sally was perfect, especially Jehu. Like a devious spider, she had spun a clever web, and I was an unfortunate fly. As I watched the sun rise outside the window, I knew I had to make Jehu see the truth.

Immediately after breakfast, I went over to his cabin.

He yawned widely when he opened the door. "Come on in," he said, his eyes bloodshot.

The table was covered in papers and melted candles, and I could hear someone snoring lightly behind a quilt at the other end of the room.

Jehu jerked his head. "Keer-ukso. We were up half the night working on this thing, and it's still not done," he said, shoving a hand through his hair. "It's a lot harder than I thought." He walked over to the stove. "Coffee?"

I nodded, and he poured two cups and brought them over to the table.

"See, Mr. Frink had some good ideas," he said, tapping the papers. "He suggested that we figure out how much money it'll take to run the mill for one year, and then ask Biddle for that, because what's the point in just building the thing if we can't afford to hire on men to run it? Keer-ukso and I are—"

"Jehu," I interrupted him. "I need to talk to you about Sally."

"Sally?" he asked, raising a questioning eyebrow.

"Sally's not what she seems," I said.

He rubbed his eyes tiredly.

"What are you trying to say, Jane?"

I took a deep breath. "I'm trying to tell you that all this"—I waved at the paper-covered table—"this whole idea of her father financing the mill is—is—," I stammered. "It's Sally's idea of a cruel joke."

Jehu regarded me for a long moment and nodded thoughtfully.

"Jane, you don't need to be jealous," he said.

"Me? Jealous?"

Jehu playfully tapped my nose. "You're the only girl

for me. Sally's just being, well, helpful."

"Helpful? Sally is just trying to get back at me. Don't you understand?"

He looked bewildered. "Get back at you? But you're friends."

"We've never been friends! She despises me. She's spent her whole life making mine a misery. Why, she's the reason I left Philadelphia!"

"I thought you left Philadelphia to marry William." He eyed me sympathetically. "Did you two have a spat?"

I groaned. I couldn't believe my ears. He didn't believe me!

He rubbed his hand through his thick black hair. "I'm doing this for us, Jane. For our future. You needn't be jealous of her."

I stared at him mutely.

"Now I have to get back to work on these plans," he said, settling into his chair, already looking down at the papers. "Maybe you can help me draw them up later? Your handwriting's much neater than mine."

How could I tell this man I loved that Mr. Biddle would never invest in a business started by a sailor and an Indian?

Finally I said, "Just don't count your gold before you get it. Anything could happen. I don't want you to be disappointed."

He ruffled my hair good-naturedly. "You worry too much, Jane."

I grew increasingly worried that William's dreams of becoming justice of the peace were not dreams after all. For as the days passed, he acquired the same luster as Mr. Biddle. Everyone wanted to talk to him because he was Mr. Biddle's chief advisor. I tried to broach the subject with Mr. Swan, but he was not the least bit concerned.

"Baldt as justice of the peace? Absurd," Mr. Swan protested. "I am one of the first men who arrived on the bay, one of the *original* pioneers," he stressed. "This is a community that values the leadership of a dedicated man, and that is exactly what I am."

"Well, it's becoming a community that values a good coin!" I said, but he just waved me away.

My suspicions were soon confirmed by Willard, of all people.

"That Dr. Baldt's gonna be the new justice of the peace!" the boy announced loudly one afternoon as we prepared supper. He was sitting at the table peeling potatoes.

"Where did you hear that?" Mrs. Frink asked.

"At Star's," he said. Star's was his new favorite spot because Mr. Staroselsky gave him a candy every time he swept the floor. From all accounts the floors of Star's fairly gleamed from Willard's enthusiasm. "I've heard lots of men saying they're gonna vote for Dr.

Baldt. Everyone's saying he's the perfect candidate."

A perfectly corrupt candidate, I wanted to say.

"But that is so odd," Mrs. Frink said, mulling it over. "Why wouldn't they vote for Mr. Swan? He's been here for so long and has helped so many of the pioneers. Dr. Baldt's been here for only a few weeks."

Willard took a vicious swipe at the potato peel. "'Cause Swan's an Indian lover!"

Spaark went still.

"What did you say?" I whispered.

"He let Keer-ukso go." He looked at Spaark and shrugged apologetically. "Everyone says Keer-ukso really stole that whiskey and some other feller got the blame. And now folks is saying that Swan ain't proper judge material!"

Spaark blinked quickly.

I looked hard at Willard. "Willard, you listen to me. Those are terrible lies, do you understand?"

"If you say so, Miss Jane." A look of shame crossed his face. "I always kind of liked Keer-ukso anyhow," he mumbled.

"I do believe I shall take a walk down to Star's. We seem to be running low on potatoes," I said, and stood up.

"But what about all these?" Willard asked, pointing to the huge bag on the floor by his feet.

My eyes met Spaark's. "I think we need a few more, don't you, Spaark?"

She nodded firmly.

As I expected, several oystermen were at the back of Star's sitting around the stove when I stepped through the door, the cheery bell announcing my arrival. I wasn't exactly sure what I was going to say to persuade the men to see reason, but I intended to say something—the very future of Shoalwater Bay depended on it.

"Miss Peck! How are you today? I have those dates you ordered," Mr. Staroselsky said.

"How wonderful. And may I have some flour, please? And one of those candies for Willard."

"Ahh, Willard. He's a wonderful boy, isn't he? So hardworking," Mr. Staroselsky enthused, moving behind the counter.

"And how is little Rose?" I asked, as I casually walked the length of the counter as if I were perusing goods.

He grinned at me. "Sleeping through the night finally."

"Wonderful," I said. "I think I'll browse a bit."

"Take your time," Mr. Staroselsky said.

I took a long, slow stroll around the store, pausing to feign interest in a bolt of fabric near where the men were drinking whiskey.

"Way I figure, we need a man who's looking out for us," one of the men said.

"Swan's a good fella, though," the other man said,

sounding reluctant. "He helped me with my claim when I first came here. Wrote it out for me and everything."

"Times change," the first man said in a hard voice.

"And Biddle's got money to burn," the third man cackled.

"Man like that will make us all rich. He knows how to get things done. Swan ain't got a head for money."

That was all too true, I thought dismally.

"Gentlemen," I said.

"Howdy, Miss Peck," one of them said.

"I couldn't help overhearing your conversation. And while I grant you have the right to your own opinions, I must tell you that I think Dr. Baldt is a very poor candidate compared to Mr. Swan," I said.

The men stared at me as if I had two heads.

"What's so great about Swan?" one of them said. "He let that Injun go free."

"I'm tired of hearing this terrible rumor," I said. "Keer-ukso did not steal that whiskey! And if you want to continue to enjoy your meals at the hotel, you would all be wise to remember that. Understand?"

They nodded their heads quickly.

The door to the back room opened, and Sally emerged, laughing. Mrs. Staroselsky followed behind her, juggling Rose. Sally was clutching a pie tin.

"Now, you must let me have a slice of that pie when it's finished," Mrs. Staroselsky said.

"But of course!" Sally trilled. "And thank you so much for your good advice."

Mrs. Staroselsky noticed me standing there. "Oh hello, Jane."

I smiled back, feeling unsettled. What was Sally doing borrowing pie tins?

Rose squirmed and Mrs. Staroselsky nodded to her husband behind the counter. "Boris will help you with the ingredients, Sally. I have to put this one down for a nap."

Sally walked over to the counter and removed a small list from her reticule.

"What can I help you with today, Miss Biddle?" Mr. Staroselsky asked.

"Let's see," Sally said, consulting her list. "One pound of flour, sugar, lard, and preserved cherries. Oh, and some cinnamon as well, please."

That was my receipt for cherry pie!

Mr. Staroselsky nodded. "Let me just go fetch that flour for you. I believe I've got more in the back." And he disappeared into the back room.

"Sally, what are you playing at?" I demanded without preamble.

"Why, Jane! How lovely to see you." She raised her basket and said innocently, "Just doing a little shopping."

The bell on the front door chimed softly behind me.

"For flour and lard?"

"Mrs. Hosmer has very kindly offered to teach me how to bake a cherry pie this afternoon," Sally said.

I stared at her in disbelief. "Mrs. Hosmer can't boil a cup of coffee, and you expect me to believe that she's going to teach you how to bake a pie?"

Sally's eyes focused somewhere over my shoulder. I turned around slowly.

Mrs. Hosmer stood there, her eyes wide.

A Rumor Rampant

Mr. and Mrs. Hosmer stopped taking their meals at the hotel.

Word soon spread, and I noticed a marked difference in the other ladies. They went out of their way to avoid me. I received more than one strange look from an oysterman at supper.

"What's this I hear about you down at Star's?" Millie asked curiously.

"What did you hear?"

"I heard that you attacked Mrs. Hosmer with a pie tin."

I groaned.

Red Charley came up to me after breakfast. "Now, Miss Peck, what's this I hear about you stealing a pie from that sweet Mrs. Hosmer? Her husband says she's been crying her eyes out."

The story was clearly growing worse and worse as it was passed from person to person. But it was Mrs. Frink's reaction that stung the most. She was my oldest lady friend on the bay.

"I didn't mean to hurt Mrs. Hosmer's feelings," I tried to explain. "It's just that Sally, Sally—" But the look on her face stopped me from continuing.

"Jane," she said, a hint of reproach in her voice. "I really don't think Sally has anything to do with this. And you don't have to apologize to me. It's Mrs. Hosmer you should be apologizing to."

"But Matilda—," I said desperately.

"I'm just a little disappointed, that's all." She sighed. "It's clear that you harbor some jealousy toward Sally, and it's hurting your friendships with the other ladies. Your jealousy of me almost kept us from being friends, remember?"

I winced at the truth. Mrs. Frink's effortless charm had threatened me so greatly when she first arrived that I had lashed out at her, jealous that she was stealing the affection of the men away from me. Even now, I felt some lingering shame at my past behavior.

In the end I decided to take Mrs. Frink's advice, and I brought a pie over to the Hosmers' cabin to try and mend the damage my words had done.

When Mrs. Hosmer opened the door, I saw Sally sitting at the table, a smirk on her face.

"I find that I've quite lost my taste for your pies," Mrs. Hosmer informed me stiffly, and closed the door before I was able to say a word.

How had I allowed myself to get into this mess? I wondered. I had played right into Sally's hands.

But, as I was soon to learn, she was not done with me yet.

The next meeting of the sewing circle was being held at Mrs. Woodley's cabin. And it was with some trepidation that I headed down the walkway the next afternoon, carrying a plate of newly baked tarts.

After careful consideration I had decided that the best course of action would be to arrive early and explain the situation to as many of the ladies who were present as I could. That way, I reasoned, I could relay my experience with Sally in Philadelphia and hopefully get some sympathy, or at least understanding. After all, they were my friends, and Sally had only just arrived.

When I got to the Woodleys' cabin, I knocked on the door, but no one answered. Clearly I was too early. I sat down on the porch and waited, nibbling on a tart. After what seemed an eternity, I started to wonder if perhaps I had gotten the day wrong.

Willard came ambling down the walkway and saw me sitting on his porch.

"Can I have one?" he asked immediately, spying the tarts.

"You may as well," I said. "They were for the sewing circle, but there's no sense in them going to waste."

"Whadya mean?" he asked. "Ma's over at Mrs. Staroselsky's right now."

"She is?"

He nodded, and I snatched the plate back. "Sorry, it looks as if I shall need these after all."

I rushed down the walkway to the Staroselskys', a feeling of relief coursing through me. But when I arrived at the cabin, I froze, hearing the rush of laughter and feminine conversation behind the door. One voice stood out from all the others.

". . . the same trouble back in Philadelphia," Sally was saying, her voice high.

Was she talking about me? I knocked on the door.

"Oh hello, Jane," Mrs. Staroselsky murmured, looking a little pained.

The other ladies abruptly ceased their conversation when I stepped into the room.

"I'm sorry I'm late," I said, breathing hard. "I thought it was being held at Mrs. Woodley's cabin."

"But I do recall telling you it was being held here, Jane," Sally said.

"I'm sure I would have remembered you telling me," I said, my voice sounding too high and loud to my ears.

The ladies stared at me.

"I brought some tarts," I said lamely.

"Uh, thank you, Jane," Mrs. Staroselsky said, and put

them on the table next to a plate of molasses cookies.

I took a seat and glanced around the circle. As I looked from face to face, no one would meet my eye. Mrs. Frink alone met my gaze, but even she looked uncomfortable.

"So," I said with forced enthusiasm. "What did I miss?"

"We were discussing the Fourth of July celebration," Mrs. Staroselsky said.

"Wonderful! I've been giving it a lot of thought, and I believe I've come up with some good ideas," I said. "Now, last year, as I may have mentioned, we held it in the clearing by Mr. Russell's cabin to accommodate the large crowd. People came from miles around. But I was thinking that perhaps this year we could have it right on Front Street. It would be beautiful, especially in the evening."

There was deafening silence.

"Well," Sally began.

All the other ladies looked at her.

"I think it would make more sense to have it at the hotel," she continued. "And make it be a ball, with official invitations, to keep the riffraff away."

"That's a wonderful idea," Mrs. Woodley gushed. "That way we can control the whiskey."

"Finally, an opportunity to wear my ball gown!" Mrs. Hosmer declared.

"But—but *everyone* looks forward to the Fourth of July here on Shoalwater Bay," I stammered.

Sally said, "All the men, you mean. This year is going to be different."

There was a long pause.

I swallowed hard. "Well, if that's what everyone wants."

"Would you care for a cookie, Jane?" Sally offered me the plate of molasses cookies. "Mrs. Hosmer made them. They're quite *delicious*," she said.

"Thank you," Mrs. Hosmer said loudly.

"I'll take another, if you don't mind," Mrs. Woodley said.

"I'd love the receipt," Mrs. Staroselsky said.

Not one person had touched my tarts.

"Speaking of food, last year we had everyone bring something to the party, and there was far too much whiskey in the end," I said with a forced laugh. "Perhaps we could draw up a menu. Spaark has been coming up with some very good receipts lately."

Another long pause.

"Oh, well, we already have a menu," Sally said.

"What do you mean you already have a menu?" I asked.

Mrs. Staroselsky looked uncomfortable. "Jane, Sally is heading up the Fourth of July celebration committee now."

"Sally?" I asked.

"I always helped Cora organize her Midsummer Gala," Sally said.

"I see," I whispered.

The air in the cabin seemed to close in on me, and I felt tears prick at the back of my eyes. I knew in that moment that everyone in the sewing circle would believe anything about me that Sally wanted them to.

"Excuse me, but I forgot that I have some important matters that require my attention back at the hotel," I said, my throat thick.

"Jane, wait," Mrs. Frink said, rising to her feet.

But I just turned and fled, tears spilling down my face.

Sally had certainly made good on her promise. She had ruined my life.

I couldn't bear to eat supper at the hotel and have to stare at Sally's gloating face, so I made my excuses and went over to Mr. Russell's cabin.

When I arrived, I found Mr. Russell sitting on his front porch cutting his toenails with a sharp knife. Mr. Swan sat next to him, writing in his diary.

"Hello, gentlemen," I said.

"Gal," the bewhiskered, buckskin-clad mountain man said, looking up from his grimy bare foot.

"Oh hello, my dear," Mr. Swan said.

"Why don't we go inside, and I'll make us some coffee?" I suggested.

I fell into my old role, boiling coffee and serving it in tin cups on the rough sawbuck table I knew so well.

We sat in front of the crackling fire, and I couldn't help but remember my very first night on the bay when I had slept in front of this same fire—aching with cold and loneliness. Now that I was at my lowest, it seemed that this filthy cabin with its odd, gruff owner was the only welcoming place on the bay for me.

"So, has business been good for you lately, Mr. Russell?" I asked, eyeing the rough wooden shelves where he stored the supplies he sold to the pioneers. They looked very full and rather dusty.

He grunted, which I took to mean *no*.

The arrival of Star's Dry Goods on Shoalwater Bay in early spring had been a tremendous blow to Mr. Russell's small trading business. Star's was a vast improvement on Mr. Russell's simple offerings of salt pork, flour, coffee, and whiskey. In addition Mr. Russell had a disagreeable habit of spitting tobacco at a person's feet, a quality that was unlikely to woo the ladies.

Mr. Swan turned to Mr. Russell, a nostalgic look on his face. "Do you remember, Russell, when you couldn't keep those shelves full for all the men coming and going? I fear those days are long gone."

"Times are changing, and not for the better, if you ask me," Mr. Russell said.

"They certainly are, old friend," Mr. Swan agreed.

Times were changing, I thought. At this rate, Shoalwater Bay would soon barely resemble the place I had come to love.

"Why the long face, gal?" Mr. Russell asked.

All the pent-up emotion rushed over me, and I began to cry.

"Gal?" Mr. Russell said.

"My dear?" Mr. Swan said, looking at Mr. Russell in alarm.

"It's Sally. She's made all the other ladies think I'm a terrible person!" I said, hiccuping.

"Does this have something to do with you, ahem, throwing a pie at Mrs. Hosmer?" Mr. Swan queried. "Really, dear girl, pies are meant to be eaten."

"See!" I wailed. "What am I going to do?"

Mr. Russell stared at me for a long moment. "You mean to tell me that you've survived out here all this time and you're letting a pesky girl get the best of you?"

When he put it that way, it didn't sound quite so bad.

A voice interrupted the quiet night.

"Obediah!"

Mr. Russell grabbed up his rifle quick as could be and stalked across to the door.

"Obediah!" the voice called again, and this time I recognized it.

The door was flung open, and Cocumb stood there, tears streaming down her face.

"What's the matter, Cocumb?" I asked.

"It's M'Carty," Cocumb said brokenly. "I think he's dead!"

or,

Mr. Swan Takes the Cake

It wasn't until some time later, after I had calmed Cocumb down with a cup of tea laced with a liberal dose of whiskey, that we heard the entire story.

M'Carty had taken his boat and gone over to Astoria as planned. However, he had scarcely been gone a day when, Cocumb said, she knew something was wrong.

It had been that still, quiet part of the afternoon when she heard the mournful cry of the owl. Everyone knows that owls do not come out during the day, but there it was—the biggest, strangest owl she had ever seen, sitting on a tree under which she and M'Carty had spent many happy moments.

An owl with eyes the exact shade of M'Carty's.

And then, mere hours ago, Mr. Dodd had seen M'Carty's empty boat drifting along the channel that led into Shoalwater Bay.

That was when Cocumb knew her husband was dead, and that the owl was his guardian spirit, or *tomanawos*, come to tell her of his tragic end.

"I know he's dead!" Cocumb insisted, her voice shaking.

After that she gave in to grief and wept inconsolably.

"What do we do?" I asked.

Mr. Russell looked at me and sighed heavily. "We look for 'im, gal."

A search party was organized for first light. All the men of Shoalwater Bay, pioneer and Indian, gathered down at the water. I joined the search as well, and we rowed up and down the bay, looking for any sign of M'Carty.

"Do you think he's dead?" I asked Jehu as we drifted along the shore, eyes scanning.

Jehu pulled the oars strongly, the hair at his neck damp with sweat. "Doesn't make sense for his boat to turn up and not him," Jehu said with the logic of a man who'd spent half his life at sea.

We searched along the bay until the tide went out, but we did not find M'Carty.

Later that night Red Charley was stumbling drunkenly along the beach when he saw a lump. Thinking it was scavenge washed ashore, he went to investigate.

And discovered M'Carty's body.

Although M'Carty was not Chinook, he had married one of Chief Toke's daughters and was much loved by the tribe. Cocumb requested that he be buried in the Chinook style.

On the day of the funeral, a large canoe was brought out. M'Carty had made this canoe with his own hands to impress Chief Toke when he was wooing Cocumb. Now Toke was burying his son-in-law in it. The long canoe, carved from a single cedar tree, was decorated with snail shells. It was one of the most beautiful canoes I had ever seen, and it was to be M'Carty's final resting place.

Keer-ukso and several of the men of the village had helped prepare the canoe. First it was scrubbed clean, and then holes were cut in the bottom to discourage anyone from stealing it. Unscrupulous pioneer men had been known to take the funeral canoes, unceremoniously dumping out the bodies.

It was a dismal gray day, the sun hidden away, as if the bay, too, mourned the passing of M'Carty. The tribe, as well as some of the original residents of the bay—including Mr. Russell, Mr. Swan, Jehu, Father Joseph, and I—were invited to the funeral ceremony. All were silent as preparations were made, and none mentioned M'Carty's name.

Grief-stricken, Cocumb refused to change her name as was the custom. This was done so that the *memelose* of the dead person would not come back and haunt you.

"I want him to haunt me!" she cried wildly, her face white. "I want him back!"

M'Carty's body, wrapped in blankets, was set in the

canoe. Then, as was customary, some of his favorite possessions were placed in the canoe with his body—a basket from Cocumb, an elaborately carved knife from Mr. Russell, and a doll from Katy. Woven mats were arranged over his body, and finally a smaller canoe was placed over it, upside down. The canoe was placed on a platform that had been built high off the ground in the woods. This was the Chinook graveyard.

Chief Toke led the tribe in a death song, one that would be sung at sunrise and sunset each day for a month. I stood next to Mr. Swan, holding Katy's small hand, watching as Cocumb sang her grief, tears streaming down her cheeks. Cocumb's weeping rose on the dark air, twining its way around my heart. Katy's eyes were red from crying, as were Sootie's. No doubt the funeral brought back memories of her own mother's recent death. We three girls had all recently lost a parent.

By the time we started back for the hotel, it had grown dark.

Cocumb, exhausted by the entire ordeal, was steered back to her father's lodge. I was going to mind Katy for a few days in order to allow Cocumb to grieve.

Katy walked silently beside me.

"Katy," I said. "My father died, too."

"He did?" she asked, eyes widening.

I nodded. "Last year. He was very sick."

Katy considered this. "Were you sad?"

"I was very sad. More sad than I can ever say." I swallowed. "I still am."

"I'm sad, too, Boston Jane," she said, tears rolling down her cheeks. And then she flung her arms around my legs and started crying in earnest.

I bent down and hugged her tight. "I know, *nika tenas klootchman*. I know."

Back at the hotel I tucked Katy into bed in my room. She was so worn-out from crying that she dropped off to sleep immediately.

I went over to my trunk and opened it and lifted out the letter from Papa that I kept among my most cherished possessions. Just looking at his familiar handwriting gave me a pang.

I missed him so much.

When I went downstairs, I discovered that all the ladies in town had pitched in to prepare a supper in M'Carty's honor. The tables groaned with the weight of the food, and people began filtering in. It seemed that the entire settlement had turned out, even men from as far away as the other side of the Columbia River. The parlor room of the hotel was soon packed, and guests spilled out all the way into the street. I circulated on the front porch, handing out tea.

Willard was glumly playing with a piece of pie instead of eating it.

"You don't like my pie?" I teased.

He swung his leg on the railing. "Is Katy gonna be okay? Now that her pa's dead and all?"

"She's very sad," I said. "But she'll be fine, especially with a friend like you to look after her."

"I'll look after her, Miss Jane," he said staunchly.

"I know you will, Willard," I said.

I left Willard to his pie and made my way back to the kitchen, overhearing a snatch of conversation.

"It ain't right. Everyone can see she's a white girl. She shouldn't be raised like a savage," a man said.

I looked over to see Mr. Dodd and his wife speaking earnestly to William.

"She needs to be with her own kind," Mrs. Dodd said in a righteous voice.

And then I could listen no more, as Father Joseph was calling for everyone's attention.

"Excuse me," Father Joseph announced solemnly. "Several of M'Carty's friends would like to say a few words." He paused. "Monsieur Russell."

The crowd grew quiet as Mr. Russell awkwardly walked up the porch steps. He looked out at the crowd and removed the wad of tobacco from his mouth and stuck it on the brim of his hat. He seemed so old suddenly, in his borrowed, ill-fitting suit.

"M'Carty," Mr. Russell began in a thick voice, "was one of the finest men I ever did know." His voice grew hoarse as he continued. "He could shoot a bear without blinking, and was as good an oysterman as they come. I reckon I'll miss him a lot." His voice grew strangled as he tried to clear his throat again.

He was silent for a few moments, but finally he swallowed hard and muttered, "Anyways, that's all I got to say right now. Thankee."

He stuck the wet wad of tobacco back in his mouth and walked back down the stairs, his head bent.

"Thank you, Mr. Russell," Father Joseph said. "Monsieur Swan?"

Mr. Swan stared out at the crowd, misty-eyed. "I find myself quite at a loss for words for once," he said, his voice trembling. "M'Carty was a good neighbor and a good friend. And, of course, he was a fine husband and father. He shall be dearly missed by all." He took a great shuddering breath and looked for a moment as though he had more to say. But then he heaved a great sigh and walked back down the steps. I daresay it was the shortest speech he had ever given in his life.

"Finally, we shall have a few words from Keer-ukso," Father Joseph said.

The crowd went still at the sight of Keer-ukso walking up to the porch. He looked out, his dark eyes bright with unshed tears.

"M'Carty was my first friend of Boston *tillicums*. He and Russell and Swan and Jane," he said, looking at me, "my friends, help me learn Boston speech. M'Carty say, 'Keer-ukso, *mika chako Boston.*' You become like Boston *tillicum*. But I tell him, 'M'Carty, *mika chako Chinook.*'

You become like Chinook." And here he gave a small chuckle. "And he married Cocumb, so I won."

The crowd laughed in remembrance.

His eyes grew serious. "But I speak Jargon best. Jargon is beautiful to tell you how I feel about my friend, because Jargon, it is Chinook and Boston speech coming together. And M'Carty and Cocumb, they are Chinook and Boston people coming together. So I say in Jargon, M'Carty, *nesayka kwansum kumtuks mika*."

M'Carty, we will always remember you.

Despite the dark cloud that M'Carty's death had cast over our little community, it was decided that the election should still be held as planned. Red Charley bowed out of the race for justice of the peace and threw in his hat for constable to fill the void.

The day of the election dawned gray and rainy, but Mr. Swan's spirits were bright.

"I was thinking that a courthouse would be my first order of business as justice of the peace," Mr. Swan said as he paced back and forth in the hotel's kitchen, where he had stopped for a bracing cup of coffee. "That way, Mr. Staroselsky wouldn't have crowds descending on his store. Maybe I can even have Jehu build it. And we can name it after M'Carty. What do you think, Jane?"

I thought he didn't have a chance of winning, but instead I said, "It's a very nice idea."

"Capital!"

163

"Mr. Swan, perhaps you ought to wait until after the elections to make any plans," I suggested.

"Whatever for, my dear?" He seemed genuinely puzzled.

I sighed.

Mr. Swan consulted his pocket watch. "Well, I must be off. Time to vote, et cetera!" He drained his cup and put on his hat.

"Good luck," I said. "I would vote for you if I could."

Mr. Swan smiled gratefully. "I know, my dear. Now, I shall see you later this evening, at which time we shall have a congratulatory toast!"

And with that, he strolled jauntily out the door, whistling to himself.

The election was held by secret ballot, and all the pioneer men cast their votes into an empty pickle barrel at Star's. Father Joseph was selected to tally the ballots. A man of the cloth, it was reasoned, could be counted on to be honest.

Men came and went to Star's as the hours passed, and Willard ran back and forth to tell us who he estimated was winning. His method of polling was quite simple. He just asked the men as they were leaving whom they'd voted for, and most of them told him.

"'Cept Jehu and Mr. Russell," he complained. "They wouldn't tell me! Lips tight as a bear trap, I tell you."

Millie had made a large iced cake for the victors.

"It looks perfectly delicious," I said.

She gave a satisfied nod. "I used nearly all of the sugar on hand for that icing. I certainly hope our Mr. Swan wins."

Late in the afternoon the whole town gathered outside of Star's and waited for Father Joseph to announce the results.

"I shall start with the winner of the election for justice of the peace," Father Joseph said, unfolding a sheet of paper. Before he could get another word out, Mr. Swan was walking up the steps of the porch, pumping hands as he passed.

"Thank you so much, my good man," Mr. Swan said to Father Joseph. He turned to the waiting crowd. "And thank you, good people of Shoalwater Bay. I promise to work very hard as your justice of the peace and . . ."

Father Joseph was tugging on Mr. Swan's sleeve.

"Monsieur Swan," Father Joseph whispered.

"Later, man," Mr. Swan said. "I'm in the middle of my acceptance speech here."

"But Monsieur Swan," Father Joseph said. "You did not win." He hesitated, clearly discomfited. "Dr. Baldt did."

Mr. Swan blanched.

"I am very sorry," Father Joseph murmured.

Looking much like a man headed to the gallows, Mr. Swan walked down the steps, pushing his way through the silent crowd. I was on the other side of the crush and I attempted to make my way toward him.

"Mr. Swan!" I called.

But he was gone.

After a desperate search for Mr. Swan, I returned to the hotel where everyone had gathered to congratulate the victors and enjoy the refreshments. Mrs. Frink had bent her rule for this one night, and everywhere I looked men were slurping down raw oysters with whiskey. No doubt she was feeling generous on account of Mr. Frink being elected our first representative. Red Charley, the new constable, was clearly enjoying himself as well and told me that his first official act would be to make a law against me being "so purty." But, in truth, it was William's night. He held court in the center of the room, with Mr. Biddle at his side, accepting congratulatory handshakes.

"Poor Mr. Swan," I said as I stood next to Father Joseph on the side of the room, watching the spectacle.

"It was a very close race," Father Joseph confided. "Dr. Baldt won by only two votes."

As the hours passed, Mr. Swan still did not appear, and I was beginning to fear the worst.

Willard was perched on a stool in the corner, eyeing Millie's beautiful iced cake.

"Why don't you go look for Mr. Swan?" I asked.

"What about the cake?" he groused.

"We're not going to cut it for a little while yet, and I

promise to save the biggest slice for you," I said enticingly.

His eyes glowed. The rascal tugged on his cap. "I'll find him. You just save me a piece of that cake."

I shook his hand solemnly. "I shall."

In the end Willard did not find Mr. Swan. Mr. Swan found us.

I was fetching tea from the kitchen when he came stumbling through the back door.

"Mr. Swan!" I cried.

But from the way he nearly fell over where he stood, I knew we were in for a bad time. He was drunk. And worse, he was on a mission.

"Good man, Baldt," Mr. Swan slurred.

"Oh, Mr. Swan," I said sadly.

He stared at me, glassy-eyed. "You tried to tell me, old girl, but I wouldn't listen, would I? No fool like an old fool."

"You're not a fool, Mr. Swan," I said.

"I am!" he said. "Most foolish man on this bay!"

"Mr. Swan," I said, taking him by the arm. "Here, why don't I take you up to one of the rooms? You can spend the night here."

He tugged his arm away from me and squinted blearily at me. "Bed? I can't go to bed! It's early! And I have to congratulate the new justice of the peace. Right thing to do."

He started ambling toward the dining room, swaying.

"No, Mr. Swan, you do not want to do that," I said

firmly. "You've had too much to drink."

"Are you saying I'm drunk, young lady?"

"That's exactly what I'm saying," I said.

"I'm not the least bit drunk. You're looking at a man who can hold his liquor."

"Mr. Swan, please, I insist," I entreated him.

He pulled away from me and marched unsteadily through the door to the dining room. I confess, I could hardly bear to watch what was going to happen next. I cracked open the door to observe the debacle.

All laughter and conversation abruptly ceased.

"Congratulations, Baldt!" Mr. Swan shouted to Mr. Biddle.

"I'm Biddle, Swan," Mr. Biddle said. He pointed across the room. "Baldt's over there."

"Oh," Mr. Swan said, and ambled his way over to William. "Congratulations, Baldt!"

William sounded a little irritated but said graciously, "Thank you, Swan."

"I say, that is a capital cake!" Mr. Swan announced with a loud hiccup.

And then there was an enormous crash.

Willard came running in the back door, out of breath. "I looked everywhere, Miss Jane, honest I did. But I couldn't find him!"

"Don't worry. I found him," I said.

"Where?" he asked.

I opened the dining-room door wide.

"Right there," I said. "Although I don't know if you're going to want any of the cake now."

Covered in icing and snoring away in the middle of the flattened confection was Mr. Swan.

CHAPTER FIFTEEN

or,

Truth and Consequences

Mr. Swan awoke the next morning in one of the hotel's beds, where Mr. Frink and Mr. Russell had managed to carry him the night before. Great gobs of icing had dried on the front of his suit.

"Where am I?" he groaned, red eyed.

"At the hotel, Mr. Swan," I said, handing him a cup of coffee.

"Thank you, dear girl," he croaked hoarsely.

He struggled to sit up. Then he looked down at his clothes, and his shoulders slumped in defeat.

"I'm a disgrace," he said, his voice empty.

"You shouldn't worry," I said lightly. "No one really had room left for cake, anyway."

He didn't laugh.

"I thought I would win, Jane. How did it happen? How?"

"Drink your coffee," I said.

He nodded morosely and took a sip.

"This is a disaster of biblical proportions," he said.

"I wouldn't go that far, Mr. Swan. But I do think things are going to be very uncomfortable around here in the near future."

"I never had a chance, did I?" he asked.

Despite myself, I smiled back at him and said, "If votes had gone to the man with the best heart, you would have won, Mr. Swan."

He swallowed hard, his eyes watery, and whispered, "Thank you, dear girl."

I was feeling thoroughly dispirited, and my mood did not improve when I stepped out onto the porch and saw William waiting for me.

"Ah, Miss Peck," he said, standing.

He seemed changed already, more confident of his power, as if becoming justice of the peace had bestowed upon him the place in society he had always desired.

"I should very much like to finish our conversation," he said.

"What conversation was that?" I replied.

"You disappoint me, Jane."

He nodded out at the muddy road before us. Already it was abuzz with activity. Horses dragging carts. Men heading out to the oyster beds. Children running and playing.

"You see, I am a man who can see the future. All

these men think of nothing but oysters and timber. They do not see what is right before them."

"And what is that?"

"Land fever, Jane. Back east, people are dying for land. With the help of Mr. Biddle, I shall create a town and sell off individual plots. Baldt City." His eyes gleamed. "It shall be the jewel of the territory if I have my way, maybe even the capital. And I shall be a rich man."

Baldt City? As ridiculous as it sounded, the crease of his brow and the set of his jaw told me William was entirely serious.

"Which brings me to you," he said, focusing on me. "Your claim is the perfect site to begin Baldt City."

"Does Mr. Biddle know about this scheme of yours?"

He laughed. "Of course, Jane. Mr. Biddle is my partner. He believes me to be an enterprising man of the highest character."

"He obviously doesn't know you very well," I muttered.

Just then, Father Joseph strolled by, Mr. Biddle at his side.

"Bonjour, mademoiselle!"

William looked around casually, then turned back to me and continued in a lower voice. "I would advise you to let me resolve this quietly. I am not unaware of your"—and here he paused to choose the correct word—

"*popularity* with the locals, and I am prepared to sweeten the pot."

"Really."

He smiled magnanimously. "In return for your cooperation, you may keep two acres of land, as well as your house."

"Two acres? But there's one hundred and twenty acres in the claim!"

William stiffened. "Do not test my generosity, Jane, or you will find yourself with no home and no land."

The future wavered before me, slippery as a muddy road.

"I should like to think about it," I said with deliberate vagueness.

"I'm a patient man, but my patience will not last forever. I am the justice of the peace now, Jane." William gave a small, thin smile. "You would be wise to remember that."

In spite of the warmth of the day, my insides felt cold as ice. William's words roiled in my stomach. My worst fears had come to pass.

Keer-ukso was in the kitchen with Spaark, and when I opened the door she blushed brightly, pulling away from him.

"Have you seen Jehu?" I asked Keer-ukso.

He pretended not to know. "Now where would Jehu be?"

"Keer-ukso! It's important!" I said.

Keer-ukso rolled his eyes. "He is at your house, Boston Jane. Where else would he be?"

I wasted no time and walked quickly toward my claim. As I rounded the bend my mouth dropped open.

My house. It was finished!

The front door opened and Jehu stepped out, looking dirty and tired.

"How do you like it?" he asked. "Finished it early this morning. I wanted to surprise you."

"It's perfect," I whispered. "It's the most perfect house ever."

And it was. It was a small log cabin with a chimney and a cedar shake roof.

He gave a satisfied nod and wiped a hand across his sweaty brow. "I was kinda hoping you'd say that. I still have a few things to do. Follow me."

As we walked around the house to the side that faced the bay, I gasped.

"A window!"

He had installed a beautiful glass window facing the water. Windows were very costly, and I could only imagine how much he'd had to save up to afford this one.

"So you can watch your sunsets," he said.

I was no longer listening to him. I was staring at my house. On my claim. But not mine for much longer. It was all about to disappear.

"You can move in anytime," Jehu was saying. "Want

me and Keer-ukso to bring your things over later today?"

I was frozen, staring back at the porch. Had I come so far only to lose everything?

"What?" Jehu asked, alarmed. "You don't like the porch? I'm gonna put up a rail, I just haven't had time to—"

"It's not that. It's William. He's the new justice of the peace."

"I heard." Jehu shook his head. "And I heard about Swan and the cake."

I twisted my hands together. "Jehu, William's going to make good on his threat. He wants my claim."

"Just put him off and try not to roil him up until my deal with Biddle's done. Then I'll take care of him."

"But don't you understand?" I cried. "Mr. Biddle is never going to give you any money! You haven't even met with him yet!"

"Sally said that the time isn't right now to bring it up with her father," Jehu said.

"The time is never going to be right! She has no intention of introducing you to her father."

"You don't know that," Jehu said in a stubborn voice.

I took his hand and looked into his eyes desperately. "Jehu, I know these people. I grew up with them. Even if Mr. Biddle did agree to meet with you, he would never partner with someone like you. He—"

"Someone like *me*?"

"I didn't mean it that way," I said quickly.

"Why? 'Cause you don't think I'm smart enough to start a business?" he asked in a dangerously quiet voice.

"No, of course not! You're very clever and talented. It's just that . . . ," and my voice trailed off.

We stood there outside the empty house, staring at each other in silence.

"It's just what, Jane?" Jehu said, and I flinched at the iciness in his tone.

I swallowed hard. "You have no connections and no references. Men like Biddle stick to their own. I'm sorry."

Jehu's face hardened, and a look I had never seen before entered his eye. "If that's how little you think of me, then I best be going." He turned and started to walk away.

"Jehu," I said, and now I was getting a little angry with him. "I'm not saying this to hurt you! Don't you understand?"

His stride didn't break.

"You'll never—"

He froze and looked back at me.

"Watch me," he said coldly.

Just when it appeared things couldn't possibly get any worse, the next morning I discovered that the sewing circle was meeting at Mrs. Hosmer's cabin that afternoon, and I had not been invited.

Mrs. Frink paused by my desk to soften the blow.

"Perhaps by next week everything will have calmed down," she suggested in a consoling voice, but I knew better. Now that Sally had her claws in the group, it would never be the same.

I tried to busy myself with drawing up a list of supplies I would need at my new house, although after a while, even that made me feel a little despondent. With William's looming threat, would I ever even have a chance to live in it?

Finally, tired of my own company, I decided to go to Star's to pick up a few things for supper. I would try out some new receipts, I decided. Baking always made me feel better. As usual, Red Charley was lolling on the barrel in front of the bowling alley when I walked past.

"See, now that I'm constable, I can put you in jail if you don't pay me what you owe me," he was telling some man.

When I entered Star's, Keer-ukso was at the counter, arguing with Mr. Staroselsky. Several men were listening to the heated exchange, Mr. Russell and Mr. Hosmer among them. Mr. Hosmer, in particular, did not seem pleased to see me.

"It does not make sense. I always buy from you," Keer-ukso said, exasperation plain in his voice.

"All I know is I'm not allowed to sell ammunition to, um, Indians anymore," Mr. Staroselsky said, sounding embarrassed.

I walked up to the counter. "Who says you can't?"

"Dr. Baldt. He says it's not allowed." He raised his shoulders awkwardly. "I can't risk it. I have a wife and baby to support."

Mr. Russell slapped Keer-ukso on the back in a consoling way. "Come on up to the cabin, Keer-ukso, and I'll get ya fixed up. I don't give a fig what the Baldt feller says. Maybe this'll even get business going again."

Keer-ukso glared at Mr. Staroselsky but went along with Mr. Russell.

"Well," Mr. Staroselsky said, patting his forehead with a handkerchief.

The front door bounced open and Mrs. Dodd stood there, a frown carved into her face.

"I'm looking for the judge," she announced to the room. "I need to speak to him about the half-breed girl."

"Do you mean Katy?" I asked. "Has something happened?"

She narrowed her eyes at me. "Not that it's any business of yours, but something's got to be done. She needs to be raised with her own kind, not with that Injun mother of hers."

I put my hands on my hips. "Really, Mrs. Dodd. You go too far."

Mrs. Dodd continued in a loud, righteous voice. "M'Carty was an honest man. He would've wanted his child raised as a white girl, not running around like some savage."

To my utter shock, Mr. Hosmer said, "What exactly are you proposing?"

"I'm willing to take her in, and she'll be a burden, but my husband and I think it's the decent thing to do."

Mr. Hosmer nodded in agreement. "Seems sensible enough to me. No point in raising the girl as a savage."

"Mr. Hosmer!" I exclaimed. "How can you say such cruel things?"

He pulled the brim of his hat low over his eyes and said, his voice cool, "Same way you can, Miss Peck."

CHAPTER SIXTEEN

or,

The Good Mother

I was sitting in Cocumb's cabin, where I had gone straight after hearing Mrs. Dodd's scheme. I had half expected to meet William along the trail, but I reassured myself that Mrs. Dodd wasn't planning on speaking to him until the morning. There was plenty of time for Cocumb to take Katy and disappear into the vast wilderness. Perhaps she could go and stay with some relatives.

But now as we sat at the kitchen table, Cocumb seemed unconcerned.

"Mrs. Dodd," Cocumb said in a scathing voice. "That woman cannot get anyone to work for her. No one likes her."

"It's William I'm worried about," I explained. "He's been waiting for an opportunity like this."

Cocumb shook her head. "I know that William is judge, but he cannot take a child away from her mother.

My father would never allow it."

"But you don't know William. He'll take Katy away just to make a point," I said. "And he can get away with it now that, that . . . ," and here my voice trailed off.

"My husband is dead," she finished.

"Yes," I replied.

"Boston Jane," Cocumb said, and I sensed a hint of pity in her tone, "you are my friend, but sometimes you worry about William too much. He's just a man."

I sighed and looked away. Across the cozy cabin, M'Carty's rocking chair sat empty in front of the fire, as if waiting for him. I couldn't help but remember the last time I had been in this room. M'Carty had been sitting in that chair. The wood gleamed in the flickering light, as if Cocumb had polished it recently.

Cocumb saw where I was looking and gave me a sad smile. "I miss him so. I keep waiting for him to walk in the door and smile at me." She closed her eyes, breathed in the air. "I feel closest to him here, where we had our life together. I couldn't bear to leave this cabin. It's all I have left of him."

The door flew open, and we both started.

Katy stood there, flush from play. Her expression grew puzzled as she took in our serious faces.

"Is something wrong, Mama?" Katy asked. "You look sad."

Cocumb hugged her daughter tightly to her bosom and smiled at me, her eyes watery. Then she looked down at Katy and smoothed the hair out of her face.

"No, *nika tenas klootchman*," Cocumb soothed, her eyes meeting mine over her daughter's head. "Everything's just fine."

It happened in the blink of an eye.

The next afternoon William appeared on Cocumb's doorstep with his new constable, Red Charley, at his side, demanding that she turn over Katy immediately. Luckily Mr. Swan was visiting at the time and managed to put him off.

"I told him that at the very least he should hold a public hearing," Mr. Swan said as he sat in the kitchen at the hotel, relaying the events. "The man knows nothing about the law."

"You'll represent her, won't you?" I asked.

"Of course," he said. "Although whether or not anyone will listen to me is another matter entirely."

Poor Mr. Swan was still taking his defeat in the election hard.

I grabbed him by the hand. "It doesn't matter," I assured him. "Don't you know that you were the best judge we'll ever have?"

He seemed to brighten a little. "I wasn't terrible," he mused.

"You're brilliant, Mr. Swan. I know you won't let William take Katy away!"

He leaped up with his old vigor, pacing back and forth in the kitchen. He slapped his hand against the table. "The rightful place for a child is with her mother!"

"Yes!" I shouted, and clapped. "More!"

"Are the Chinooks any less deserving of their own children?" he boomed, as if he were already in the courtroom.

"Bravo!"

He nodded to himself, rubbing his beard thoughtfully. "It shouldn't be too hard, I should think. Just have to get my thoughts in order."

"Wonderful, Mr. Swan. Is there anything I can do to help?" I asked eagerly.

"Actually, might I have a piece of pie? A man can't think on an empty stomach."

The day of the hearing arrived, and it seemed as if every pioneer in the territory had packed into Star's Dry Goods to watch the spectacle. Our esteemed new constable, Red Charley, was covertly taking bets on the outcome on the porch outside.

I managed to find a seat on a bench near Cocumb, Katy, Mr. Swan, and Mr. Russell.

Mr. Swan did his best to calm Cocumb's fears. "This is all quite preposterous, my dear lady," he told her. "And I can assure you that I shall not allow your lovely daughter to be taken from you."

Cocumb sat numbly clutching Katy, who was entirely confused by the situation.

"I don't want to live with Mrs. Dodd," Katy said in

a clear voice. "Willard says she's mean."

Mr. Swan smiled kindly. "And you shan't have to, my girl." He turned to Cocumb. "I shall be calling both you and Mr. Russell to the stand to testify as to M'Carty's wishes regarding Katy's upbringing."

"Can they win?" Cocumb asked in a nervous voice.

He patted her on the hand. "You have nothing to fear."

I scanned the room of eager spectators. Mrs. Dodd and her husband had taken prominent seats up front. Behind us, Father Joseph, Auntie Lilly, Spaark, Keer-ukso, and Chief Toke sat. On the other side of the room were the Hosmers, and Mr. and Mrs. Frink, and even Mr. Biddle. Jehu was sitting next to Sally, and he did not meet my eyes.

The doors to the back room of Star's swung open. William strode through and took a seat at the very same table where Mr. Swan had once presided. He didn't need to bang on his table with a pipe for order, the way Mr. Swan once had. He simply looked out at the room, and it quieted down of its own accord. I looked over to gauge Mr. Swan's reaction. He had gone a little pale.

"We are here today," William began, hands crossed, "to discuss a concern raised by Mr. and Mrs. Dodd. It is their contention that Katy, the child of M'Carty, should be removed from her mother and raised by someone in town. Mrs. Dodd, would you care to state your case?"

"I sure would," Mrs. Dodd said, her face set.

With exaggerated importance, Mrs. Dodd walked

up to an empty chair at the front of the room.

"It's one thing to live near the savages, or even work with them," Mrs. Dodd said, staring at Cocumb. Cocumb stared right back at her. "But it is quite another to allow a white child to be raised by a savage. It ain't right. She should be raised with her own."

There were soft murmurs of assent from the assembled audience.

"I should like to add," William said, "that this concern has been seconded by other members of the community. Now, as this procedure was requested by Mr. Swan, I shall hear his arguments at this time."

Mr. Swan stared around at the crowd, looking uncomfortable and tugging absently at his collar.

"Mr. Swan," I hissed. "Go!"

He lumbered up, clearing his throat. "Good neighbors," he began, "this is a simple matter that concerns a family. Now, many of you knew M'Carty well, and as he is unable to speak for himself in these proceedings regarding his intentions for his only child, Katy, we shall hear testimony from M'Carty's friends, as well as his wife. Mr. Russell?"

Mr. Russell walked up and took the chair recently vacated by Mrs. Dodd. He spit a wad of tobacco. It landed with a wet slap at Mrs. Dodd's feet.

"M'Carty loved Cocumb. He loved her people," he said.

Cocumb smiled at him gratefully.

He stared at Katy. "And he loved that little girl like

he was a crazy fool. Thar ain't no way he woulda wanted her taken away from her mama."

"But her education is being neglected!" Mrs. Dodd shouted.

"That little girl's smart as a whip. She speaks English and the Jargon. And jest who are ya anyhow to be talking about educating? I don't see ya got any children of your own. Seems to me that ya wouldn't know the first thing about being a mama. How many languages you speak?"

Mrs. Dodd went white.

"And the rest of ya. Mind yer own business, I say."

Mr. Russell got up and ambled back down into the audience.

"Thank you, Mr. Russell, for your expert testimony," Mr. Swan said with an approving smile. "As most of you know, Mr. Russell was M'Carty's best friend. Now we shall hear from M'Carty's wife. Cocumb?"

"Indian lover!" someone shouted from the back of the room.

I whirled around in my seat, but found myself staring at a roomful of stone-faced men and women, some of whom I had once counted among my friends.

Cocumb just stiffened her back and walked regally to the witness chair.

"My husband is dead," Cocumb said in a clear voice. "All I have left is my daughter. My beautiful Katy. She is part Chinook, part white. If it matters to you, I plan to raise her knowing the customs of both peoples."

"Why should we listen to a savage Indian?" Mrs. Dodd's husband barked.

"I am her mother," Cocumb said quietly.

"Thank you, Cocumb," Mr. Swan said, and helped her back to her seat.

Mr. Swan drew a deep breath and looked out at the room. "It has always been my opinion that mothers are most perfectly equipped to care for their children. I do not think anyone in this room or in society shall disagree with me on this basic point. There is no legal reason to remove Katy from Cocumb's care. She should remain with her mother, where she belongs."

A hush fell over the room.

"Very well, Mr. Swan," William said. "I find that your arguments have no merit in this matter."

"It is a matter of law, sir," Mr. Swan blustered.

William raised an unconcerned eyebrow. "Really? Which law? I believe this matter falls under my province as justice of the peace. As M'Carty once said, we make our own laws out here."

I couldn't take it anymore. I leaped to my feet. "You're married to an Indian! How can you say such things? What if Katy were your daughter?"

There were stray murmurs of surprise in the room. It seemed that William hadn't told all his new constituents about his own marriage.

William tensed, and then an icy calm seemed to

settle over him. "Miss Peck, my affairs are none of your concern, and you are lucky I am in an agreeable mood or I would have you jailed for contempt." He inclined his head. "But as you have mentioned them, I would be more than happy to speak to your concerns."

I held my breath, and to judge from the silence in the makeshift courtroom, so did everyone else.

"In the first place, as you well know, my wife is only half Indian. But let us set that aside. In the event of my untimely death, I would be only too happy to have a suitable member of society raise my offspring, otherwise the child would revert to savagery. Therefore, I hereby declare that Katy shall be removed from her Indian mother and given into the care of a pioneer lady, to be raised as a civilized child." He nodded to Red Charley. "Constable."

"No!" Cocumb cried.

Chief Toke stood up, Keer-ukso behind him.

But Red Charley already had latched his beefy hands around Katy's arms and was dragging the struggling child from the room.

"Mama!" Katy called.

"Mr. Swan! Do something!" I shouted over the furor.

Mr. Swan looked at me helplessly as Cocumb sobbed into my shoulder.

A True Lady

The late days of June brought bright blue skies and cool evenings but no solace. Everyone went about their lives as if the terrible incident with Katy had never occurred. Except it had. I had only to walk over to Toke's lodge and see Cocumb's stunned face to know that.

Sally spent her days in the hotel parlor, making endless plans for the upcoming Fourth of July celebration. Even Mrs. Biddle got involved. Now, instead of endless complaints, she had endless demands.

Each morning she met me with a list of meticulous requirements, none of which, naturally, I was able to fulfill. There were no orchestras on Shoalwater Bay, nor were there any theater troupes, or hot-air balloons to hire, or any form of entertainment besides drinking, gambling, and bowling.

"Miss Peck," she said after I informed her that the special coconut macaroons she requested would take months to arrive. "I am most disappointed in you."

I wanted to tell her that she wasn't the only one. The ladies of the sewing circle were disappointed in me. Jehu was disappointed in me. Mrs. Frink was disappointed in me. Only Brandywine, the dog, seemed happy in my presence. But he left fleas on my bed.

I took to spending all my spare time in my house, walking the floors and measuring the windows for curtains. It was my refuge from the hotel—and the disturbing sight of Sally Biddle holding court in the parlor. Her gay laughter was a grating reminder of everything I had lost—my friends, my place in this world, and, I feared, Jehu.

Jehu, for his part, seemed determined to prove me wrong about Mr. Biddle. By all accounts he spent every waking moment refining plans for the mill and lobbying Sally. It was as if he and I were living in separate worlds, like ships passing at sea. I often saw him strolling with Sally down the road, head bent in conversation, or outside Star's with other men. Once, his blue eyes met mine and held.

And then he looked away.

One morning the last week of June found me at my house as usual—only this morning I had awakened there.

I had moved in at last, with the help of Mr. Frink and Mr. Russell. The house was most beautiful in the early morning, when the warm light washed over it like watercolors. I saw Jehu's hand in every detail, from the well-laid floors to the gleaming table that stood in the center of the room. I glanced out the window, admiring the view.

A figure was walking across my claim, and I felt a rush of fear. William?

Except he wasn't walking. He was running, which the dignified William would never deign to do. And he was far too small to be William, anyway.

The front door banged open, and there stood Willard, breathing hard. Brandywine ran into the house in front of him.

"I been looking everywhere for you!" Willard exclaimed.

"Is that so?" I asked. "You know very well you are supposed to be at the hotel helping Millie and Spaark."

He shook his head. "You gotta come with me."

"Willard," I said. "What have you done now?"

"I ain't done nothing." He gave me an exasperated look. "It's Katy!"

My heart fell. "Katy?"

"Them Dodds, they're treating her real bad. Making her do the laundry and make the soap. She's like a slave or something!"

"How do you know all this, Willard?" I asked.

He stared at his booted foot. "On account of the fact that I been spying on them."

Now *that* I could believe.

"Honest. I ain't lying, Miss Jane," Willard pleaded.

I looked into his eyes, the eyes of a scamp and a pie thief.

"All right, Willard," I said, holding out my hand. "Show me."

Willard, it turned out, was quite an accomplished spy. No wonder he always knew when a pie was cooling on a windowsill.

He led me up a little path through the woods that backed onto the Dodds' small cabin. There was an open window in the back of the house, and through it wafted the strong smell of unwashed clothes.

"Come on," Willard whispered. "They're around the side of the house making soap."

Making lye soap was an arduous process. But more than that, it was a dangerous job. It required pouring boiling water over wood ashes, adding fat, and then stirring the whole stinking mixture for hours on end.

And that was exactly what Mrs. Dodd was making Katy do—stir the boiling pot. She had clearly been at it for some time, for the poor child seemed close to dropping from fatigue. Her small hands had raised red welts on them from where the burning liquid had splashed from the pot.

Mrs. Dodd came out to inspect.

"Is it done yet?" Katy asked in a small voice.

Mrs. Dodd slapped Katy hard on the arm, and beside me Willard flinched as if he had been struck, too.

"Ow!" Katy said, tears springing to her eyes.

"What did I tell you about not speaking unless spoken to, girl?" Mrs. Dodd growled.

Katy whimpered.

"Get back to your stirring or they'll be no supper for you again!"

Willard and I crouched in the bushes and watched as Katy stirred the boiling lye, a long, slow tear crawling down her smudged face.

When I returned to the hotel, I searched out Mrs. Frink. Surely she would be sympathetic, no matter what Sally had said about me.

She was at her desk, writing a letter.

"Excuse me, Matilda? May I have a moment of your time?"

Mrs. Frink rubbed her eyes. "Of course, Jane. What is it now?"

"Actually, I just came from Mrs. Dodd's house," I began. "She's treating Katy terribly. We must do something."

"Jane," Mrs. Frink said, her tone measured. "I'll grant you that Mrs. Dodd can be difficult, but I can't imagine she'd be deliberately cruel."

"But she is!" I exclaimed. "I saw it with my own eyes. It's clear to me that the only reason she took Katy was so she wouldn't have to pay any more help."

Mrs. Frink looked off into the distance. "Perhaps Katy's just having trouble adjusting to her new life."

"She needs to be with her mother. Think of Cocumb! Please, you of all people must understand how awful it is to lose a child."

Mrs. Frink's face whitened at this.

"Something must be done," I said. "People respect your opinion. They'll listen to you."

"Jane," Mrs. Frink said, clearly torn. "It's an unfortunate situation, I agree, but William's the judge. He makes the law now."

"He's horrible and you know it!" I shouted in frustration. "He doesn't care what happens to Katy. How can you stand by and watch this happen and not do anything?"

Mrs. Frink said in a helpless voice, "Even if I were to challenge him, I have no doubt that he would prevail. And nothing would be accomplished by that. Perhaps we should just wait awhile and see what happens. Maybe Katy will come to like living with Mrs. Dodd."

"I can't believe you're saying this," I said, and started to walk away before I said something else I would come to regret.

"Jane," she called.

I turned back.

A look of uneasiness flitted across her face, and then she shook her head. "I'm sorry."

"So am I."

Mr. Swan was even less helpful than Mrs. Frink.

He removed his spectacles and wiped them on his coat. "Perhaps it's a good idea, after all, Jane. William has been telling me about Governor Stevens and his plans for the region. We all have to face facts eventually, dear girl. And the fact is that many of the Indians in this territory are destined for reservations." Mr. Swan stared at me, a little sadly it seemed. "Just as I am destined to leave this place."

"Leave?" I gasped. "But how? Why?"

He pulled a packet of letters out of his coat pocket and handed them to me reluctantly. They were neatly tied with a ribbon. The return address was Boston.

"My wife," he explained. "She wants me to come home."

I stared at the letters and wondered at the family he had left behind.

"But what about our oyster beds and all your plans?"

He waved at Shoalwater Bay.

"This was only ever destined to be an adventure for me," he said, and then cleared his throat. "My life awaits me in Boston."

"When will you go?" I asked.

"After the Fourth, I should think."

"I'll miss you, Mr. Swan," I said quietly.

He smiled at me, his eyes wet. "And I shall miss you as well, my dear."

As I mulled over the news about Mr. Swan's imminent departure, I decided to go and see if Mr. Russell could help me. After all, the brash mountain man had never cared much for other people's opinions of him.

He wasn't in his usual spot on the porch when I arrived. I peeked into his cabin. It seemed to be in an even greater state of disarray than usual. An immense pile of laundry was stacked in the corner. Scraps of old food, scattered across the table, were being enjoyed by all manner of vermin, and the place was simply bursting with fleas. Even Brandywine wouldn't go inside and sat on the front porch whining.

I finally found Mr. Russell in the cowshed, milking Burton.

"Hello, Mr. Russell," I said.

His beard seemed to have gone gray overnight, and his face was thinner than when I'd last seen him. He had taken the death of M'Carty very hard, I knew.

"Are you well, Mr. Russell?" I asked hesitantly.

He spit a wad of tobacco. "Why wouldn't I be, gal?"

"It's just that you were—I mean—that M'Carty was—your best friend here on the bay," I stammered.

His hands froze and his face went still in a mask of grief.

"That he was, gal," he said, his voice hollow. "But I can't bring him back. Nobody can. It's just best to keep on going. It's really the only thing to do."

"Oh, Mr. Russell," I said, laying a hand on his shoulder.

He shook it off. "Shouldn't ya be at the hotel, gal?"

"Actually," I said, "I thought I'd tidy up the cabin, if that's all right with you."

He shrugged. "Suit yerself, gal."

I spent the rest of the day cleaning Mr. Russell's cabin and making him a proper meal. He appeared to have been living on some particularly old and rotten-looking venison and onions. After he had cleaned his plate and was sitting in front of the roaring fire, pipe in hand, I broached the subject of Katy with him. His expression didn't alter as he stared into the fire.

"So what should we do?" I asked when I was finished.

Mr. Russell simply stared into the fire, his expression morose.

"What's the point, gal?" he muttered, his voice tired.

"But they're mistreating her!" I shouted. "It's intolerable!"

"I can't do anything by myself, gal," Mr. Russell said. "Baldt's in charge now. His word's law round here."

I knelt in front of him, holding his hands. "Things are changing, yes. But we mustn't give up hope. Not yet."

"I'm an old man, Jane, and I'm tired. I jest want to

go and find somewhere quiet to live out the rest of my days. It's getting a bit too busy around here for my taste. Think I need a change."

"Not you, too!" I exclaimed.

"What do ya mean, gal?"

"Mr. Swan's leaving!"

"He's a smart fellow to get out while the gettin's good," Mr. Russell said.

"Am I speaking to the same man who assured me I had nothing to fear from William?"

But Mr. Russell didn't respond. He just stared into the fire.

Supper at the hotel that evening was unbearable.

I deliberately did not sit at the head table, preferring the company of a group of scarcely washed oystermen to that of Sally and her parents.

"Evening, Your Honor," someone said.

I looked up to see William stride through the door, circulating around the room like royalty.

Mr. Russell's words rang in my ears.

Baldt's in charge now. His word's law round here.

And I knew that Mr. Russell was right after all.

The drizzly rain that greeted me the next morning washed away any lingering reservations I had about what I must do.

As I walked down Front Street and saw Mrs.

Woodley's girls playing happily in the mud of the road, my resolve grew stronger. When I finally reached the Dodds' cabin, I stood on the porch for a long moment. From inside came the clear sound of Mrs. Dodd berating Katy.

"You stupid child!" she shouted. "What'd I tell you about not letting the iron rest too long!"

This was followed by a loud slap. I knocked firmly on the door.

"Who is it?" Mrs. Dodd demanded.

"Miss Jane Peck," I called.

The door flew open.

"My man dropped the laundry off yesterday," Mrs. Dodd said.

"Actually," I said, pressing forward, "I believe you forgot to return something to us."

She flushed and her face scrunched up. "If it's that glove you're talking about, I told you I ain't got it."

But I ignored her and walked straight into the appalling little cabin. Her husband was nowhere in sight. Thank heavens.

Katy saw me and her eyes lit up. I gave her a quick smile of reassurance.

Mrs. Dodd blustered, "Now see here, you can't just go walking into my house—"

Before she could finish her sentence, I claimed Katy in an easy swoop. The little girl clung onto me as if for dear life.

"Hey!" Mrs. Dodd shouted, regaining her anger. "You can't take her. The judge gave 'er to me!"

"Not anymore," I said.

"You can't do this!"

"Watch me." I paused in the doorway and turned back. Katy's arms tightened around my neck. "And by the way," I said, "we shan't be requiring your services any longer."

As I strode down the street, Mrs. Dodd chased after me, shouting, "She's giving Katy back to her Injun mother! Stop her!"

I didn't break my stride but kept moving down the walkway. People opened the doors of their cabins to see what the commotion was all about, and oystermen stopped in the street, setting down their baskets. Red Charley hopped off his barrel and walked toward me.

Mrs. Dodd flew past me down the muddy street to Star's, hollering, "Judge! Judge Baldt!"

The door to Star's opened and William walked out, followed by a small crowd including Mr. and Mrs. Staroselsky, Mrs. Woodley, and Mrs. Hosmer.

"What seems to be the problem?" William asked.

"She's taking the girl!" Mrs. Dodd shouted at my back.

"Miss Peck!" William called in an authoritative voice, and I froze and turned to face him. "Before I have you arrested for kidnapping, may I ask: What exactly are you doing?"

Katy eyed the gathering crowd fearfully. "Run, Boston Jane!" she whispered.

"It's okay," I whispered back. I looked at William. "I'm taking Katy home!" I said in a defiant voice.

"See!" Mrs. Dodd shrieked.

"Miss Peck," William said. "Why do you insist on defying me at every turn? By now you surely must have learned that you can't possibly win."

Mrs. Dodd pressed her case. "She's mine, Yer Honor. You gave 'er to me!"

William shook his head in irritation and snapped to Red Charley, "Constable, give the child back to Mrs. Dodd."

Red Charley stepped forward, a little apologetically. "Sorry, Miss Peck, but I am the constable now."

I held up a warning hand and he hesitated.

"Dr. Baldt, you specifically said that Katy was to be given to the care 'of a lady.'"

William's eyes narrowed, but he gave a short nod of his head.

"To a *lady*," I said. "And you, Mrs. Dodd, are no kind of lady."

Mrs. Dodd became enraged. "How dare you—"

"I do dare," I said, advancing on Mrs. Dodd. "A lady would never do this to a child." And I pushed up one of Katy's sleeves.

A collective gasp went through the crowd at the sight of the livid bruise on Katy's arm. Mrs. Woodley put her hand over her mouth and tugged her daughters close. Mrs. Staroselsky cradled Rose tight to her bosom. Even Mrs. Hosmer went a little pale.

"The girl wouldn't mind me," Mrs. Dodd said quickly. "You can't let her do this!"

I stared at William. "You are the judge, Dr. Baldt. If your intention was to give Katy a good home, then I can assure you that I have one. I am quite prepared to raise her."

William looked uneasily at the crowd that was now regarding Mrs. Dodd as if she were a bug. I had won!

Then William cleared his throat. "Miss Peck. You are an unmarried girl. You are not a suitable mother for the child."

My heart sank. Katy's arms clutched me even tighter.

"But I am," a voice rang clearly from the back of the crowd.

Mrs. Frink stood there, a look of calm composure on her face, her husband a step behind.

"I am a married lady, and I am more than willing to take Katy in. Do you have any objections to me, Dr. Baldt?" she asked with just a trace of sarcasm in her voice.

William hesitated a moment too long.

"What you got against Mrs. Frink?" one of the men shouted angrily.

"Yeah, Baldt," another one hollered.

Even Red Charley seemed to eye William suspiciously.

The crowd began to rumble, and William's mouth tightened.

"I would be most delighted if Mrs. Frink took in the child," William announced.

"That's more like it," Red Charley said.

Mrs. Frink met my eyes and smiled.

She was, as I had always known, a true lady.

or,

The Claim

On the third day of July all of Shoalwater Bay was busy with preparations for the next day's celebration, and the staff of the hotel was in full swing.

Spaark, Millie, Mrs. Frink, and I gathered early and worked hard all day. Even Willard showed up on time for once and did as he was told. It seemed that I was his hero now that I had stood up to Mrs. Dodd, and it was all he talked about as he peeled his potatoes.

"You should've seen the look on that mean old Dodd's face when Miss Jane got Katy!" he said, describing the scene in detail again and again.

Mrs. Frink had given Cocumb a permanent room at the hotel so that mother and daughter could be together until the fuss with Mrs. Dodd died down. Cocumb wasn't as upset about moving out of the cabin as I had thought she would be.

"It was getting lonely in that cabin all by myself," Cocumb admitted.

The festivities were to be held in the downstairs of the hotel. As promised, Sally had given official invitations to Willard, to be hand-delivered several days before.

I had not received one.

As we were short staffed, I lent a hand with the cleaning. I dusted and swept clumps of mud that criss-crossed the carpet in spite of the boot scraper at the entrance. As I straightened up the settee in the parlor, I came upon a small book wedged beneath a pillow. I recognized it at once.

It was Sally's copy of *The Young Lady's Confidante*, our textbook from the Young Ladies Academy.

I idly flipped through the chapters: Conversation, Deportment at the Dinner Table, Receiving and Returning Calls, Pouring Tea and Coffee, and lastly, Being a Good Guest. Clearly Sally had never paid much attention to that chapter.

And then from among the pages of the chapter entitled The Great Mistake, a folded piece of paper fluttered to the ground. I picked it up and unfolded it. The penmanship was Sally's distinctive swirling hand.

Dear Cora,

I hope this letter finds you well. As for me, things have not improved in this wretched place. It never stops raining, and my best dress is quite ruined.

Everyone is excited about this ridiculous Fourth of July party that I have agreed to organize for them. It is very tiresome and hardly worth the trouble, although it should provide some small amusements. Where else shall I see drunkards and fools dressing up like gentlemen? I rather doubt that any of them will be able to read the invitation! The ladies are not much better.

Mrs. Staroselsky, whose husband is a shopkeeper here, is responsible for ordering all the fabric. She has horrible taste, and I daresay that the scullery maids of Philadelphia look like ladies in comparison to the rags she chooses. And she is not even the worst.

Mrs. Woodley, who has five ill-behaved brats, spends all her time eating. She can barely tie her corset, she is so nauseatingly fat. Every time I see her I am reminded of a pig.

The best of them, Mrs. Hosmer, has proved to be so tedious that I find myself making up stories in my head when I am forced to listen to her conversation. And she fantasizes that she is a cook—a cook! How laughable.

The proprietress of the hotel, Mrs. Frink, imagines that she is running a first-rate establishment. In fact, her tastes are—how shall I put it? I think "vulgar" and "low class" perfectly describe them. Our lodgings are cramped and filthy—barely fit for animals—and she lets just <u>anyone</u> stay here.

As I mentioned before, I have been enjoying myself

immensely by toying with pathetic little Jane Peck and
her deckhand sweetheart . . .

I stood there staring at the rest of the letter, her cruel words lingering in my mind.

After a moment I started to put the hateful letter back between the pages of the book . . . and then hesitated. I walked over to Mrs. Frink's desk and slipped it between the pages of her ledger.

Later that afternoon Sally came wandering downstairs, her eyes scanning the room.

"Are you looking for this?" I asked in an innocent voice. I held the book out to her.

She hesitated and then snatched it from me.

"Where did you find it?" she snapped. "I've been looking everywhere for it."

"It slipped behind a pillow."

"Oh," she said, and then leafed through the book, her face growing more anxious. Finally, in what looked like desperation, she turned the book upside down and shook it.

"Are you missing something?" I asked.

"Uh, no," she said uneasily, and walked away.

Later that night, after supper, I was alone in the kitchen experimenting with a new receipt for oysters when the back door opened, and I looked up to see Mr. Russell standing there.

"Gal," he said, tipping his hat and spitting in the

same instant. He held out a tin bucket.

It was full of fresh-picked strawberries.

"Figured you could make one of them pies of yours with 'em," he said, pulling up a bench.

"Thank you, Mr. Russell," I said. "Would you care for some coffee?"

He nodded and I poured him a cup, adding the milk and sugar I knew he favored. The mountain man took a long sip and cracked a smile at me.

"Sure is better than that first coffee you made," he said with a chuckle.

When I had first arrived on the bay, I had mistakenly ground coffee beans in a grinder that had been used to grind peppercorns. Needless to say, it had produced a fiery brew.

Mr. Russell sat there for a long moment, looking down at his cup.

"Heard what ya did for Katy, gal," he said. He looked up, and I saw the admiration in his eyes. "I'm proud of ya."

"Thank you," I said.

"Anyhow, I jest came to say good-bye. I'm leaving day after tomorrow."

"You can't leave!"

"I'm an old man now, gal," he said, his face shadowed with a lingering sadness. "M'Carty and me, we came here together. I can't rightly see stayin' here with him gone."

"But Mr. Russell," I said urgently. "Please don't leave

here. I'd miss you so. We all would. You're the heart of this place."

"I'm ashamed of myself," he whispered, his voice bleak. "For not standing up for Katy. For not taking care of her like I promised M'Carty I would."

"Then stay and remind her every day what a wonderful father she had. Be the father he can't be. I know you can do it," I said. "After all, you've been like a father to me."

Mr. Russell's mouth trembled, and he nodded shortly.

Finally he said, "Reckon there's a thing or two I could teach her."

"Just as long as you promise not to teach her how to spit," I said, and winked.

It was late when I finally finished cleaning up in the kitchen. I hung up my apron and, taking a lantern, made my way toward the parlor. The events of the past few days had left me quite exhausted, and I was looking forward to a good night's sleep.

"Miss Peck," William said.

I was so startled, I nearly dropped my lamp.

William and Mr. Biddle were ensconced on the settee, papers strewn out before them.

"Please join us, Miss Peck," William said.

My eyes flicked to the papers. They looked very official.

"It's very late, and I—I was just leaving to go to my

house," I stuttered. "I have a long day tomorrow."

"Ah, what we wish to discuss may have some bearing on that," William said in a voice that brooked no refusal. "Now please sit."

I closed my eyes. I had known this moment would come, hadn't I? I forced myself to sit down in a chair across from them.

"Ahem," Mr. Biddle began. "Now, William here was telling me that there has been some . . . confusion . . . as to the legitimacy of a very agreeable claim."

"Confusion?" I asked.

William gave a mock-weary sigh. "Miss Peck has been perpetrating a fraud." He waved my claim in front of Mr. Biddle.

Mr. Biddle narrowed his eyes at me. "Is this true?"

I stared at him wordlessly.

"I'm sorry to say that I fear your father would be most disappointed in you," Mr. Biddle said. "A young lady's place is in the home. Married. Not out on the frontier, running about like a hellion, and cavorting with savage Indians. And now this business with the claim. You are meddling in men's work. It has gone on long enough."

"But it's my home!" I gasped.

"Not anymore," William said. "It was never a legitimate claim, and therefore we are seizing it."

I closed my eyes. It was over.

"You're not taking anything from anyone, Baldt," a voice said mildly.

Jehu stood in the doorway, his blue eyes glinting in the candlelight.

"Mr. Scudder," Mr. Biddle said, "this matter does not concern you."

Jehu walked into the room and stared at the two men. "I reckon it does concern me. Seeing as Jane here's the woman I love."

I gasped.

"That claim you're holding is legitimate," Jehu said.

William snorted balefully.

"Legitimate?" Mr. Biddle said, sounding irritated. "My good man, I fear your feelings have overshadowed your judgment."

Jehu shook his head. "That claim isn't Jane's."

"I could have told you that," William snapped.

"It's her father's," Jehu said softly.

"What?" Mr. Biddle asked, startled.

"Dr. Peck never came out here," William said, his voice strident. "I would have known, I—"

My eyes blinked open and I stared at Jehu in confusion.

"He didn't have to." Jehu gave me a gentle smile, his eyes shining. "Being a sailor and all, I spent a lot of time in Philadelphia." He chuckled self-consciously. "I admit I got into a scrape or two back in those days. Fact is, I became acquainted with a surgeon who treated a lot of sailors. Turns out that gentleman was James Peck."

Across the room Mr. Biddle was looking from

William to Jehu, as if taking the measure of each man.

"Papa's best clients were sailors," I said. "You know that, William."

Jehu nodded in agreement. "Dr. Peck was one of the finest men I have ever been acquainted with. At his request I filed a claim for the land in his name. I acted as his agent in this matter. It was James Peck's claim. And now that he's dead," Jehu said, looking at me steadily, "it's Jane's."

It was as if the room fell away and he was as I had first seen him—standing on the ship, the blue sky bright behind him, his hair shiny as a crow's wing.

"Do you have any proof of this?" William sputtered.

Jehu pulled a folded piece of paper out of his coat pocket, opened it, and placed it on the side table. "That's Dr. Peck's signature granting me authority to act as his agent."

I looked at the document and my father's signature at the bottom. Bold and strong as he had been.

James Peck

Mr. Biddle studied the paper and narrowed his eyes at William. "This *is* James Peck's signature."

William was on his feet. "I don't believe this for a second. It's a charade!"

Jehu stared at him, his gaze steely. "I don't rightly care what you believe, Baldt. Fact is, a man who lies to a young lady to get her to come to the frontier for his own greed and then abandons her ain't worth spit."

Mr. Biddle's eyes narrowed on William. "I thought you said Miss Peck broke off the engagement."

"She did," William insisted weakly.

"Only because you were already married to another woman! Or did you forget to mention that to Mr. Biddle here?" Jehu drawled.

The moment stretched out.

"I see," Mr. Biddle said coolly, eyeing William with something approaching distaste. "If Mr. Scudder says he brought the letter from Dr. Peck, I am inclined to believe him. I suggest you let the matter drop." He turned to me. "You must please accept my apologies, Miss Peck. I was a great admirer of your father. This claim is clearly yours. I don't believe we have any further business to discuss."

William slumped back into his chair, defeated.

Afterward I grabbed Jehu and hugged him hard.

"Did you really know Papa?" I asked. Was it possible? Had he been one of those sailors who had stumbled drunkenly onto our doorstep to have his head stitched up all those years ago?

Jehu chuckled and said, "Let's just say I heard stories about a surgeon who had a red-haired daughter who liked to jump on sailors' bellies."

or,

A Memorable Day

The Fourth of July dawned as bright as the bay itself.

We began setting up at daybreak, with all the guests at the hotel lending a hand, except, naturally, Sally, who was spending her morning getting ready for the big event. I could only imagine what she was going to wear.

Jehu and I had stayed up late the previous evening discussing the future. After his attempt to take my claim, it was pretty clear that Mr. Biddle was not going to finance the mill.

"What will you do now?" I asked.

"I'll go to San Francisco and look up Johnson," Jehu said with a good-natured shrug. "The old man's bound to know someone who can help us." Captain Johnson was Jehu's old boss.

Now as I worked in the kitchen, loading food onto platters, I hoped that Jehu would be able to find someone to finance the mill. The back door opened, and the next thing I knew, I felt myself enveloped in a furry embrace. I pulled away and looked up at the face peeking out from the cape.

"Mr. Hairy!"

"Howdy, Miss Peck," the unrepentant thief said. Hairy Bill's eyes alighted on a platter piled high with fried chicken. "Hmm, that sure looks mighty tasty."

I smacked his hand away. "That is for the party this afternoon."

He pulled his face. "I'll never make it till then. I'll die of starvation!"

I shook my head and pushed the plate toward him.

"Where have you been?" I demanded as he immediately began to demolish a chicken leg.

"Here and there," he answered as he gnawed at the bone.

"Mr. Hairy!"

"I been staying at Jehu's cabin," he muttered.

"Jehu's cabin?" I stared at him with dawning realization. "It wasn't Keer-ukso snoring. It was you!"

He looked down at his plate. "Could be."

"But why were you hiding out at Jehu's cabin?" I asked.

Hairy Bill pulled a face. "Come on now, Miss Peck. I show up in town and whiskey gets stolen. Who do you think they're gonna blame, huh? Why, I bet even *you* thought it was me."

"I did not," I protested, feeling ashamed of having thought that very thing.

"Didn't hurt me none to lay low for a while, and besides, I helped finish that house of yours." He reached in his pocket and tugged out a letter. "Oh, this is yours."

I turned the envelope over in my hand. It was my letter from Papa, the one that had been in my trunk. I stared at my father's signature for a long moment.

"Mr. Hairy," I said, suspicious. "You didn't have anything to do with my claim, did you?"

"Now where would you get an idea like that?" He blinked at me innocently. "You know I can barely write out an I.O.U."

"I suppose so," I said, turning away.

And then he chuckled and murmured, "But I sure can copy good."

Even though I had not received a formal invitation, I would still be attending the festivities. As concierge of the hotel I was responsible for overseeing the food. I wore my gold silk dress and arranged my hair.

Sally, never one to be outdone, swept downstairs wearing a magnificent blue dress with flounces of scalloped lace, her blond curls arranged to perfection.

She looked around the parlor with irritation.

"Why has nothing been set up as I directed?" she snapped at Millie. "The tables are supposed to be inside."

Millie shrugged. "Mrs. Frink said to set up outside."

I watched as Sally flounced out to the front porch, where Mrs. Frink was directing the men.

"Mrs. Frink," Sally said, her tone sharp, "what is going on? I distinctly recall deciding that the tables were to be set up inside."

Mrs. Frink pursed her lips at Sally. "Yes, well, I felt that your plans were a little . . . how shall I put it? Vulgar and low class. So I have made a few changes."

Sally paled a little and then turned on her heel and walked back into the hotel.

The rain stayed away and the day grew warm, sultry even. People began arriving, and not just those people who had been on Sally's guest list. It seemed as if the entire territory had turned out for the celebration.

"Willard," I asked. "Exactly how many invitations did you deliver?"

"None," he confessed sheepishly. "I forgot."

In spite of Willard's forgetfulness, or perhaps because of it, the Fourth of July celebration drew a large crowd. Chief Toke and his tribe arrived, bearing strings of salmon. Mr. Staroselsky delivered a huge barrel of pickles. Fresh oysters were piled high on one of the tables, and for once I found them delicious. Perhaps they were like Shoalwater Bay: an acquired taste. To no one's surprise Red Charley rolled out several casks of whiskey.

William was nowhere to be seen, having left town rather urgently on business for the governor, or so he had told Mr. Frink.

"Good riddance," Millie said.

Chief Toke came up to me during a quiet moment.

"Boston Jane," he said, putting his hand on my shoulder. "Thank you. For my granddaughter."

"It wasn't me. Mrs. Frink was the one who saved the day," I protested.

He looked me in the eye. "You were the one who stood up to William, and that is what matters."

"Maybe next year we can get Mr. Swan elected to replace him. I don't see why you shouldn't have a vote," I added with a laugh. "Or me either, for that matter."

"I shan't be running," Mr. Swan said from nearby, almost teary eyed. "This is my last Fourth of July on the bay."

"You should write a book, Mr. Swan, to remember it by," I suggested.

"What a capital idea! Perhaps I can even make some money on it," he said, his voice excited.

"Be sure to put me in it," I said.

"Of course, dear girl," he promised.

Sally, clearly put out that her plans were not being adhered to, sat at a table on the porch with her mother beside her, waving her fan and looking faintly irritated.

I was standing at the table where the food had been laid out, getting myself a cup of tea, when the ladies from the sewing circle arrived. Sally immediately walked over, as if she were the hostess of the party.

They were talking among themselves, but I could hear them clearly.

"Hello, ladies!" Sally declared in a shrill voice.

Mrs. Staroselsky's eyes flicked over Sally's dress. "What a charming ensemble, Miss Biddle."

"Why, thank you," Sally said, preening.

"I can't imagine that I should even know how to order fabric so pretty," Mrs. Staroselsky declared. "After all, I have horrible taste."

Sally looked startled but quickly recovered. "Why don't you all get something to eat and then join Mother and me at our table."

"The cake looks delicious," Mrs. Woodley said, and then stared hard at Sally. "But perhaps I shouldn't eat it. I wouldn't want to get any fatter."

Sally swallowed hard and smiled brightly at Mrs. Hosmer.

"Mrs. Hosmer, do come join Mother and me," she said.

"I'm so sorry, Sally," Mrs. Hosmer said. "But I wouldn't want to bore you with my tedious conversation."

Sally went so pale that she looked as if she were about to faint.

Quite undone, she whirled around and ran straight into me, spilling my tea all over her fine dress.

We both stood there for a long moment, and then Sally sobbed and ran into the hotel.

Mrs. Staroselsky came up behind me, carrying Rose. "Tut tut, such a clumsy girl."

"And not very nice at all," Mrs. Woodley added.

"We are all so very sorry, Jane," Mrs. Hosmer said sincerely, taking my hands. "Please forgive us."

"Of course," I said. "And I am so very sorry for saying you didn't know how to cook."

"Oh, but I don't," she said with a self-deprecating laugh. "My husband hasn't had a decent meal since we stopped coming to the hotel. The poor man is wasting away."

I laughed.

"But I should very much like to learn how to cook," she continued. "That is, if you are still willing to teach me. I promise to be a better pupil."

"I'd be honored," I said.

When the sun set, torches were lit along Front Street, turning the muddy road to magic. A group of men pulled out their fiddles and began playing a merry tune. Men grabbed ladies and swung them around. I watched as Mr. Frink gently led Mrs. Frink out to dance.

Keer-ukso whirled me around.

"I like this Boston custom," he grinned.

The song ended and people clapped and cheered.

Mr. Swan walked to the porch of the hotel and shouted for silence.

"I do believe a speech is in order on a day such as this," he began, looking out at the crowd. "As you all know, I have spent three years on this bay, and tomorrow I return to Boston. But I tell you now that I have never known such good and true friends as the ones that I have made here," he said, his eyes resting on mine. "I shall miss you all dearly."

The crowd roared in approval.

"Now, I believe another member of our community would like to say a few words," he said. "Jehu?"

I watched as Jehu walked up the porch, hat in hand.

"I reckon we should thank Mr. and Mrs. Frink for organizing such a good spread," he said, and the crowd immediately cheered.

He looked out at the crowd, his eyes searching and then coming to rest on me. "I'm not too good at giving speeches, but this is one I've been practicing for some time." He took a deep breath. "Jane Peck, will you be my wife?"

I imagined I felt a draft from the collective in-rushing of breath. All eyes were focused on me. I had no doubt that I was blushing from the tips of my toes to the crown of my head.

Jehu walked down the steps, his eyes intent. The crowd parted to let him through until finally he stood before me, the blue-eyed sailor of my dreams. The scar on his cheek twitched in the nervous way I knew so well.

"Well, Jane?" he asked gruffly. "Will you have me?"

I looked into his blue eyes, eyes that had seen me come so far.

"Marry him, gal!" Mr. Russell shouted.

As Papa liked to say, you make your own luck.

"Yes!" I shouted.

The crowd erupted into a great cheer, and Jehu picked me up and swung me around in his arms, kissing me soundly on the lips.

"Yer jest marrying her for her pies," Red Charley said sourly.

I looked into Jehu's laughing eyes.

"Well, are you?"

Jehu winked. "Could be I am."

For one brief, shining night Shoalwater Bay was as I had known it could be.

Everyone danced and ate and sang, and Brandywine stole so much food, his belly fairly sagged. Jehu spun me under the starry sky, and the night air turned cool, but I was warm clear down to my bones. The warmth I felt came not from the bonfire but from the love of my friends, who looked on in approval.

Father Joseph and Auntie Lillie tapped their feet, watching as Mr. Swan took a turn with Cocumb. Keer-ukso held Spaark to his chest, pressing a gentle kiss to her forehead. And Willard, the rascal, danced with both Katy and Sootie. But it was the sight of Mr. Russell gallantly spinning Millie, his eyes alight with mirth, her blush becoming, that made us all smile.

Oysters and dreams may have brought us here, but something else had made us stay. This place at the edge of the wilderness was now our home. And as I looked up at the sky, the scent of the bay sweet all around, I knew that nothing would ever be easy. The rains would return and mud would clog the roads, and William would cause trouble, but in the end we would try our best. Here in this place, far from finery and corsets, ladies spoke their minds and followed their hearts.

Who knew what the future held—indeed, who ever knew?—but in the arms of the man I loved, I had nothing but hope.

The next morning the whole settlement came down to the beach to see us off to San Francisco. Jehu was going to try to find Captain Johnson, and I was going to buy fabric for a wedding dress.

"The sewing circle is finally going to get some sewing done," Mrs. Staroselsky said.

"We shall make you the most beautiful wedding dress ever," Mrs. Hosmer promised.

The schooner dropped anchor, and a rowboat was lowered.

"Have you got the list?" Mrs. Frink asked.

"Of course," I said. She wanted me to purchase

some things for the hotel. A concierge's duties were never done.

A rowboat touched the beach, and a man came walking up to us, carrying a bag of mail.

"Any of you know who Miss Jane Peck is?" he asked, scratching his head.

"Who doesn't?" Mr. Swan said with a low bow to me.

The man presented me with an envelope. The return address listed Papa's solicitor in Philadelphia. I scanned the contents and looked up at Jehu.

"It appears I have found you an investor for your mill," I said mysteriously.

"Who?"

"Me! My inheritance is waiting for me in San Francisco, and it should be more than enough to help get your mill started!"

"Huh," Jehu said.

"Naturally my investment shall be on the same terms that you would have given Mr. Biddle," I said. "And I shall insist on being a full partner."

"Partner, eh?" Jehu pretended to consider my offer seriously.

"Well?" I asked.

Jehu grinned at me. "You drive a hard bargain, Miss Peck."

"You could say that I'm a woman who knows what she wants," I said.

Keer-ukso slapped Jehu on the back. "Good thing

you are marrying her!"

We were getting ready to get in the rowboat when Katy and Sootie came running down to the beach, Willard hot on their heels.

"Wait! Boston Jane!" Sootie shouted.

The children ran up to us.

"It's a present for you," Katy said shyly, handing me a flour sack.

I pulled out a miniature handmade canoe with two little dolls sitting in it. One had red yarn for hair, and the other had yellow yarn.

"I made the boat," Willard said proudly.

"What's that stick?" Jehu asked.

"It's the paddle," Sootie said.

"I'm assuming that the doll with the red hair is supposed to be me. But who is the doll with the yellow hair supposed to be?" I asked.

"Better not be Baldt," Jehu muttered.

I laughed.

"We couldn't find any black yarn," Katy explained.

"Either way, gal, I reckon it means we're expecting you and Jehu to go places," Mr. Russell said, and spit.

As we stood at the rail of the schooner, watching sunlight skip across the shimmering water and the sleek sea otters frolic between the waves like playful puppies, Mr. Russell's words hummed in my ears.

Jehu slipped his arms around me. In the distance,

Shoalwater Bay was disappearing, my house now a speck on the cliff.

The ship lurched suddenly, but Jehu's arms held me steady.

"You're not gonna puke, are ya?" he teased me.

I looked into his laughing blue eyes and smiled.

"If I do, I'll aim for your boots."

I looked across the stretch of water, bright and shining as hope, and knew that Mr. Russell was right. We were going places.

But we would be back.

The End . . . for now!

AUTHOR'S NOTE

The town where Jane lives is based on two early oyster settlements, Bruceport and Oysterville, on Shoalwater Bay (now known as Willapa Bay) in Washington State. During its heyday in the nineteenth century, an estimated 50,000 baskets of oysters were shipped off the bay every year. These settlements boasted hotels, dry goods stores, churches, and taverns, as well as coffin shops. But like many boomtowns, Bruceport disappeared, and Oysterville now has only a remnant of its former glory. My own family was very involved in the oyster trade on Shoalwater Bay. My great-grandfather, Charles Holm, and my grandfather, Wendell Holm, and my uncle, Ivan Holm, were all oystermen. Like Jane, I have come to appreciate oysters.

Cocumb's experience in *Boston Jane: The Claim* was

inspired by the real-life story of Bill M'Carty, or "Old Brandywine," one of the original oystermen on Shoalwater Bay. According to James Swan's account of the incident in his book, *The Northwest Coast, Or, Three Years' Residence in Washington Territory*, M'Carty fell off his boat and drowned, leaving behind an Indian wife and an eleven-year-old daughter called Katy. Upon M'Carty's death, Katy was taken away from her mother and placed in the custody of the family of a local judge. Her mother managed to regain custody of her for a time but, sadly, in the end was strongly pressured to give Katy into the keeping of a local pioneer family. Tragically, James Swan approved of this action and was, in fact, instrumental in the removal of the child. Unlike in *The Claim*, there is no mention of the child ever being returned to her mother.

Elections for constable, justice of the peace, and representative to the legislature were in fact held in 1850s Shoalwater Bay, although in general, rough-and-tumble pioneer justice prevailed. James Swan echoed this concept by noting, "For what did we want of laws? We were a law unto ourselves." One of the first trials to be held there was over stolen whiskey.

William Baldt's get-rich-quick land scheme of Baldt City was inspired by the real-life dreams of Elijah White, a former physician turned Indian agent, who promoted and sold nonexistent land plots in an imaginary place called Pacific City to unknowing settlers.

The Frink Hotel is loosely based on the Stevens

Hotel in Oysterville, which housed oystermen. Isaac Whealdon, an early settler on the bay, commented thus on the hotel and its gracious owners:

> It is said of him and his wife that they never turned away a man who was hungry and cold and I, who came here an orphan boy, say Mrs. Stevens gave me the first feather pillow and bed mattress I ever had. When we used to sit down to that long old table, in that old dining room where Mr. Stevens did the carving and Mrs. Stevens poured the coffee, I used to look at them and say to myself, "God bless you!"

Likewise, Star's Dry Goods was inspired by the Jewish dry goods stores that existed on the frontier in the nineteenth century, and Staroselsky and Rose Star are family names.

RESOURCES

Chinook Tribal Office, Chinook, Washington.

Ilwaco Heritage Museum, Ilwaco, Washington.

Pacific County Historical Society and Museum, South Bend, Washington.

Oysterville: Roads to Grandpa's Village, Willard R. Espy, University of Washington Press.

The Northwest Coast, Or, Three Years' Residence in Washington Territory, James G. Swan, University of Washington Press.

Also by Jennifer L. Holm

Jane Peck enrolls in Miss Hepplewhite's Young Ladies' Academy to turn herself into the perfect bride for her childhood idol, William Baldt. But when William's marriage proposal strands Jane in the Pacific Northwest—with no fiancé in sight—she must learn to survive the wilds of the new frontier on her own.

Hc 0-06-028738-1 • Pb 0-06-440849-3

In this second book of the Boston Jane trilogy, Jane Peck is forced to make a new home for herself in the rugged nineteenth-century Washington Territory after she's abandoned by her fiancé an ocean away from her native Philadelphia. A perilous manhunt and a blossoming romance lie ahead.

Hc 0-06-029043-9 • Pb 0-06-440881-7

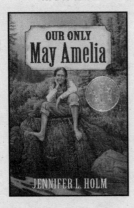

A Newbery Honor Book

With seven older brothers and a love of adventure, May Amelia Jackson just can't seem to abide her family's insistence that she behave like a proper young lady. She's sure she could do better if only there were at least one other girl living along the banks of the Nasel River. And now that Mama's going to have a baby, maybe there's hope.

Hc 0-06-027822-6 • Pb 0-06-440856-6

www.harperchildrens.com
www.jenniferholm.com

🏛 HarperCollins*Children'sBooks*

🏛 HarperTrophy®
An Imprint of HarperCollinsPublishers